Pilate's Wife

ALSO BY H.D.

Pilate's Wife

H.D.

Edited, with an Introduction,
by Joan A. Burke

A NEW DIRECTIONS BOOK

Book and cover design by Erik Rieselbach
Manufactured in the United States of America
New Directions Books are printed on acid-free paper.
First published as New Directions Paperbook 890 in 2000
Published simultaneously in Canada by Penguin Books Canada Limited

Library of Congress Cataloging-in-Publication Data
H.D. (Hilda Doolittle), 1886–1961
Pilate's Wife / by H.D. ; edited and with an introduction by Joan Burke.
p. cm.
ISBN 0-8112-1433-8 (acid-free paper)
1. Procula, Claudia–Fiction.
2. Bible. N.T.–History of Biblical events–Fiction.
3. Governors' spouses–Palestine–Fiction.
4. Pilate, Pontius, 1st cent.–Fiction.
5. Jesus Christ–Crucifixion–Fiction.
6. Women in the Bible–Fiction.
I. Burke, Joan A.
II. Title
PS3507.O726 P5 2000
813'.52–dc21   99-059104

New Directions Books are published for James Laughlin
by New Directions Publishing Corporation
80 Eighth Avenue, New York 10011

INTRODUCTION

Although H.D.'s critical reputation has relied more exten-
sively on her poetry–particularly the earliest *Sea Garden*,
which solidified her reputation erroneously as an Imagist,
and later *Trilogy, Helen in Egypt,* and *Hermetic Definition*–
her creative impulses were again and again directed toward
prose compositions throughout her nearly fifty productive
years from 1912 to 1961. She wrote in several genres and experimented blending poetry and prose, ultimately producing
fifteen surviving novels and novellas, considerable short fiction, translations of classical Greek drama, and several essays,
including the expanded *Notes on Thought and Vision*. In 1924,
H.D. began writing *Pilate's Wife*, a work she was not to complete until 1929. Chronologically, it stands as H.D.'s sixth
novel, after *Paint It Today, Asphodel, Palimpsest, Hedylus,* and
the destroyed novel, *Niké*.[1] A number of her novels have recently been issued or re-issued, but this edition marks the
first publication of *Pilate's Wife*.

After revising the 168-page manuscript of *Pilate's Wife* in
December 1934, H.D. mailed it from London to Ferris
Greenslet at Houghton Mifflin. Greenslet summarily rejected it, claiming that the American public would find it
"harder reading than *PALIMPSEST*" and that he personally
found *Pilate's Wife* lacking "quite the intensity of emotion
that made [*Palimpsest*] so memorable."[2] Greenslet's brief rejection seemed to close the door on the possibility of future
publication, H.D. never resubmitted it; but twenty years

later, perhaps after Greenslet's rejection lost much of its sting, she began to "re-read" it. In twelve days of reading—over a period from May 1954 to August 1957—she made several hundred hand-written revisions on the typescript. As a result, *Pilate's Wife* now stands as a novel of two periods, a cross-generational hybrid of sorts, substantively written by H.D. in her late thirties and early forties, but reworked by her when she was approaching her seventies.

Often referred to as the third of H.D.'s "history novels," after *Palimpsest* and *Hedylus*, *Pilate's Wife* adds an obvious biblical dimension. The novel supports Alicia Ostriker's assertion in *Feminist Revision and the Bible* that among the women poets and novelists of the twentieth century, "H.D. is the most profoundly religious, the most seriously engaged in spiritual quest...."[3] In many of her later prose works, H.D. explains her personal and literary goals within a religious context. One of these works is the autobiographical text, *The Gift*, about her Moravian upbringing in Pennsylvania, in which she addresses the spiritual "gifts" she inherited matrilineally and patrilineally. In an enlightening passage from *The Gift*, H.D. relates her father's method of naming her: "My name was Hilda: Papa found the name in the dictionary, he said. He said he ran his finger down the names in the back of the dictionary, and his finger stopped at Huldah and then went back up the line to Hilda." The proximity of "Hilda" to the Old Testament prophet "Huldah" is obviously more than an alphabetical coincidence for H.D. Even as a child, she felt she was the "inheritor" of a gift she could not understand, one whose "expression [...] was somewhere else. It lay buried in the ground in older countries, fragments of marble were brought to life again after long years." The full force of H.D.'s prophetic gift lay buried, waiting for her encounter with the mythical worlds of Egypt, Greece, and Rome.

The Gift, however, is not the only place H.D. writes about her religious and literary calling. In *Tribute to Freud*, another World War II composition, she compares herself to two other Old Testament figures as she relates a session in which she and Freud discuss her dream-identification with the Doré biblical illustration, *Moses in the Bulrushes*. H.D. writes of her confusion over the conflicting prophetic models of Miriam and Moses:

> The Professor and I discuss this picture. He asks if it is I, the dreamer, who am the baby in the reed basket? I don't think I am. Do I remember if the picture as I knew it as a child had any other figure? I can't remember. The Professor thinks there is the child Miriam, half concealed in the rushes; do I remember? I half remember. Am I, perhaps, the child Miriam? Or am I, after all, in my fantasy, the baby? Do I wish myself, in the deepest unconscious or subconscious layers of my being, to be the founder of a new religion?

Interestingly, Freud remembered the witnessing Miriam "stood afar off" from Exodus 2.4; she is not present in Doré's illustration. In a characteristic gesture, reinforcing her contention that "the Professor was not always right," H.D. resists Freud's insistence that she identifies with the silenced, barely visible Miriam. In the years during and following World War II, H.D. found herself more and more consciously addressing the urge to be that "founder of a new religion." But many years earlier, her preoccupation with religious topics had already begun to emerge. Thirty years before she completed *Helen in Egypt*, H.D. was at work on *Pilate's Wife*. This "new religion" to which H.D. had always dedicated her writing life, even unknowingly, is a spiritual and poetic one, spoken by and about women but also speaking as Moses did, "mouth to mouth" with the divine.

A consideration of H.D.'s revisionary agenda is nothing new; her oeuvre is dedicated to dismantling the patriarchal paradigms which have restricted women's participation in all aspects of culture, most notably, as far as I am concerned, in religion. No one would have agreed more than H.D. with Helene Cixous' call for a resurgence of woman-centered studies through which we can re-examine and rebuild our pasts.[4] H.D. constantly looked backward and saw both women and men in that historical crowd. Even when women had been erased, silenced, cast as diminutive figures in western mythology over the centuries, H.D.'s characters from classical sources show that spiritual inheritance has always been bestowed by fathers and mothers.

H.D. puts powerfully articulate women back into the socio-religious myths, but many of the stories H.D. has re-envisioned are those which have become secularized over thousands of years. Spiritual matters in them, posing no threat to present orthodoxy, can simply be glossed over in favor of the highly-charged narratives of the gods and their mortal counterparts. Certainly there is no extant religious tension in a reading of *The Iliad* or *The Odyssey,* or Euripides' *Helen* or *The Women of Troy.* When H.D. reconfigures these texts as new myths, as she does in her later work, she puts women in secular and intellectual territory. This is not to say that her revisions lack revisionary force. Clearly a character like Helen has force as a debilitating cultural symbol. The impact of *Helen in Egypt* is profound, but not because of an inherent anxiety with its precursive content.

The content in H.D.'s *Pilate's Wife,* however, is much more immediate, more culturally pertinent, and thus more potentially subversive—the New Testament legends of Christ's Crucifixion and his resurrection after death. For her choice of material, H.D.deals with troubled biblical narratives. The several stories of the transfiguration and the resurrection in the Gospels and elsewhere in the New Testament do not agree upon just how prominent women were in the so-called "Jesus movement."[5] In a bold maneuver, clearly one that Ferris Greenslet recognized in 1935, the nearly seventy-year-old text of *Pilate's Wife* poses a genuine feminist encounter with Christianity at an uncertain, perhaps its most vulnerable, theological moment. With the exclusion of "Christ as the universal scapegoat of human sin," as Northrop Frye has identified the gospels' essential metaphor, both the complicit guilt prompted by his death and the promised redemption his death insures for his followers are held in serious question.[6]

Pilate's Wife offers a woman-centered rendering of the Crucifixion story, even though its title also suggests objectification and anonymity. When we begin the novel, therefore, we rely on what we know from the bible: an amorphous female character presented in rather traditional, paternalistic terms. Of the four main gospel authors of the New Testament, only Matthew mentions the wife of Pilate, and briefly. In Matthew 27.19, after Jesus is arrested and brought before her husband, she sends him a crucial message, telling of her recent dreams and warning him to treat the prisoner as a just man. Even though Matthew makes it clear that Pilate's wife has been afforded no actual speaking presence in the Jerusalem court, has been permitted no real influence in shaping the outcome of this debate, she is nevertheless a presence. She is an unnamed character whose very silence would have provoked H.D.'s imagination. In this biblical precursor, Matthew's shadowy wife of Pilate could certainly be seen as a visionary, a dreamer who implicitly trusts her visions and is courageous enough to send her message into a political arena from which she herself is excluded.

Although H.D. claims in the novel's "Author's Preface" that she has honored the "traditional rendering of the Gospels," she has, instead, taken a single line from one gospel, imaginatively enlarging it. As a result, we have the consuming search of the Roman wife of Pontius Pilate, now named. She is searching for a divinity she can recognize, a search which greatly minimizes the life and the teachings of the Jewish poet-prophet. The story begins indeterminately a few days, perhaps a week or two, before Jesus's arrest; but even mentioning Jesus at this point significantly misrepresents the nature of H.D.'s re-telling. The story of Jesus does not control her narrative. Pilate's wife is a serious woman engaged in her own spiritual quest long before she has heard about or encountered Jesus; and her search continues to be central after he leaves her world. H.D. makes her new focus very clear in the most blatant way, by erasure. In *Pilate's Wife*'s expanded narrative, a woman's self-directed quest is for a life-affirming "feminine counter-part of deity," supplanting the messianic focus of the New Testament.

In *Pilate's Wife*, H.D. downplays her intention to change the face of divinity. In her one-page prefatory "Author's Note" she claims her only wish is "to re-establish the familiar scene"; but she goes on to justify the liberties she takes with the central character's name: "I could not materialise my central figure, Pilate's Wife, under her historical or traditional name, Claudia Procula. However, a Roman lady, of that class, might have had a dozen names, and Veronica might have been one of them." It is not surprising that assertions and doubts about Veronica's name literally frame the events of this book. According to Ernst Cassirer, making the "word" synonymous with "flesh," as the bible does, is common to all mythology:

"[…] that the potency of the real thing is contained in the name—that is one of the fundamental assumptions of the mythmaking consciousness itself."[7] By selecting the name Veronica to "materialise" Pilate's wife, H.D. knew she would be echoing the traditional stories of the legendary Saint Veronica who, on the road to Calvary, offered Jesus a handkerchief to wipe his face. Later she discovered that she had carried home a perfect image of his face imprinted on her cloth. According to Ewa Kuryluk's *Veronica and Her Cloth*, all three—the woman, her cloth, and Christ's face—are conflated as true images in "fusions and confusions, typical products of magic and mythology which never stop associating one thing with another…."[8] "Veronica" now stands for any representation of the face of Jesus, particularly one on cloth.

By erasing the historical Claudia Procula and superimposing "Veronica"—a palimpsest overtly laden with religious association—H.D. makes clear that in the Roman Veronica will be found the divine face. The novel's first sentence emphasizes the importance of her name: "Names held small part in her consideration, yet she spelled her own arduously, sensing in its hard and pebble-like lustre, some unknown element." Later what is "unknown" can be seen, when Pilate occasionally calls her "Vera-ikon" because he has long relied on the truth of her judgments. H.D. further highlights Veronica's visionary "astuteness," comparing her to a "prophetess," even though she has not come to see herself as one, certainly not one called to speak any truth about herself or about religious issues.

Pilate's Wife begins in Veronica's ornate boudoir within the palace—it is "a cold room, like its mistress," "a dead room"—one in which Veronica's former lover, Memnonius, tells her "You have not risen." All human interaction here is initally dead; her passion for both Pilate and her male lovers is gone;

and the narrator acknowledges that Veronica is "always a little out of step with the processions she was, of necessity, part of." In contrast to this enervating human activity is positioned Veronica's pet, whose "vivid presence" actually gives definition to the room. As he flies from curtain to curtain, the animal, ostensibly a small monkey, assumes many identities: "a cat or a marmot," "an insect," an "owl with wings folded over downy feathers"—truly an "odd creature" whose eyes have given him a reputation for possessing "some eternal and complicated wisdom." The creature is made more exotic and strange by being named "Bes," after a minor Egyptian god associated with "rest, and joy, and pleasure" and often depicted in royal rooms where childbirth occured.[9] In Veronica's "tomb," then, are two imprisoned animals: one a lively exotic beast who jumps up at whim; the other, a constrained wife, a woman who has been conditioned to chatter away like "some half-tamed wild-bird." She is a woman who is almost dead.

Veronica's journey toward resurrection is persistently marked by questions and confusion. As part of her quest, she visits the mountain temples where women pray to Isis; but while Isis "flamed her imagination," she finds the mutilation of Osiris disturbing. Talking to Fabius Nobilior, her current lover and a military general in Pilate's service, Veronica hears about the Cult of Mithra, but finds its restrictive emphasis on brotherhood problematic. There is no doubt, as she says, that "it leaves out women." To help propel her search, the Egyptian Memnonius convinces her to visit a young psychically gifted woman who is likened, in one of the book's many androgynous similes, to a "priest." Initially resistant but soon enchanted by this woman named Mnevis, encouraged by her prediction of "a complete change, spiritual, emotional, physical," Veronica begins to experience "sudden pre-vision[s] of inner splendour," during which she realizes "that her outer kingdom and her inner sanctity, had some link missing." Veronica is motivated by her personal inner quest, but also mesmerized by Mnevis as a seer and eventually as her "ideal sister."

Actually the name "Mnevis" for this second woman in *Pilate's Wife* is equally rich in etymological association. In addition to the fact that "Mnevis" rhymes with and echoes "Isis" and Jesus," the first of its two syllables, Mne-, is a rare three-letter sequence reserved for words related to memory. (Mnemosyne is the goddess of memory and mother of the Muses.) The second syllable is the past participle of the Latin verb, *videre*, to see. It also evokes the face or appearance; thus in a number of ways Mnevis's name is related to seeing memories or actually representing memory's face. The placement of the verbal components might also function as a symbol of the remembering process. Finally, the two syllables frame a nearly complete "EVE," a visible but inaudible presence in the center of the seer's name.

Eventually Mnevis begins to share statements she had heard by a new teacher, one who believes women have an important place in the "spiritual hierarchy." Veronica is able to use his wisdom to bring forth her own visions, so that "Every phrase of the Jew opened a door." About halfway through the novel, as she remembers more clearly the forgotten goddesses and women of religious prominence like Lilith and Eve, Veronica begins to feel alive. Furthermore, she knows she "didn't want death, really. She wanted an answer." By the end of Chapter VI (with only a third of the novel remaining), Mnevis tells Veronica that "the man they–they all adored, [is] in danger," and Veronica offers to use her influence to help him.

Helping the troubled Jew obviously (and finally) takes us into familiar New Testament territory. Veronica fails to act on this plea for assistance until later, when she experiences a waking/dream vision in which she is "called" by name. She answers this call consciously by rising from her bed and making her way to the window, from which, looking below in the courtyard, she sees a man being led by a group of soldiers. The man held there is, "it was obvious, replica of her dream" and not only that, he also has "the face of her little [Etruscan] sun-god" prayed to during her childhood. In Veronica's waking integration of dream and reality, both past and present, the two stories of resurrection intersect. Thus it is that in the last sixty pages, Veronica's narrative meets and ends up determining the story of Jesus.

On the final pages of *Pilate's Wife,* Veronica sees that the deepest reclamation of her divine self requires an inordinate amount of concentrated effort and may also demand action. In this regard, her spiritual conclusions are antithetical to the physical/sexual ones of Jesus or "The Man" in D. H. Lawrence's *The Man Who Died,* which was begun in 1927, and published in 1931, the year after Lawrence's death. Both these novels of the 1920s generally recast the same legends of Christ's resurrection; in both versions Christ is crucified but he does not quite die on the cross. A joint consideration of these contemporaneous texts reveals their differences and the early depth of H.D.'s radical expansion of conventional Christianity, but the comparison hardly constitutes the first intersection of H.D. and Lawrence, either critically or biographically.

In several works, H.D. and D. H. Lawrence addressed or fictionalized the other. After reflecting on her friend Stephen Guest's comments when he brought her a copy of *The Man*

Who Died, H.D. realized that she may have been the model for Lawrence's priestess of Isis.[10] Lawrence, as well, may have been H.D.'s model for Jesus, the young bearded Jew whom she describes as "too slight" and "sort of a poet." (Without question, he is Rico in H.D.'s later thinly disguised roman à clef, *Bid Me to Live.*)

During World War I, Frieda and D. H. Lawrence lived for a while with H.D. and her then husband, Richard Aldington. An overwrought H.D. had recently suffered the stillborn death of her first child, and Richard, then a soldier and home only periodically from France, was having an affair with Arabella Yorke, who lived in the flat above theirs. During this time H.D. became infatuated with Lawrence, and he became enchanted with her. In a 1916 letter to John Cournos, H.D. speaks of being taken with, but sometimes fearful of Lawrence's "distant passion"; about the same time, Lawrence praises H.D. as a woman on "the threshold of a new world, or underworld, of knowledge and being."[11] Although their actual relationship was never a physical one, and lasted only three years (1914–1917, with a sporadic correspondence which ended in 1919), the tension between them lasted for much of H.D.'s life.

That the two revisionary texts here testify to our century's gender war is irrefutable; obviously the "Man" and "Wife" in the titles forecast opposing approaches. Their publication histories alone speak volumes. When H.D. first learned from friends that Lawrence had worked on this theme, she thought, "Now he has taken my story," since she had discussed it long before starting its actual composition in 1924.[12] Certainly the battle between these two texts involves gender privilege, and is intensified by a religious and literary tradition that has persistently resisted women writing about sacred matters, particularly if they are resurrecting pre-Christian feminine faces of the divine.

A glimpse at the concluding passages from *The Man Who Died* shows us how differently H.D. and Lawrence portrayed characters and events in their biblical narratives. At the end of Part I, the "Man" misleads the women concerned for his safety by saying he "must go to my Father," but this deception holds a profound truth. For all its semblance of a revisionary tale, he is returning to the old world and the ways of his fathers. In Part Two, he journeys to the temple of Isis, vaginally represented by "the dark stain of blood in its end groove." The "Man" finally builds his life on "the deep-folded penetrable rock of this living woman! The woman, hiding her face. Himself bending over, powerful and new like dawn." It is only in this apparent sexual conquest that he is able to experience his resurrection, claiming " 'I am risen!' " The following are his last words (and the last words of Lawrence's novel):

> I have sowed the seed of my life and my resurrection, and put my touch forever upon the choice woman of this day, and I carry her perfume in my flesh like essence of roses. She is dear to me in the middle of my being. But the gold and flowing serpent is coiling up again, to sleep at the root of my tree.
>
> So let the boat carry me. To-morrow is another day.

It is no accident that sowing seed and "resurrection" are closely yoked in Jesus' life, the future envisioned as the novel ends. The proverbial "serpent" is resting now, lodged at "the root of [his] tree" to be awakened when he will "put his touch" on another "choice woman" whom he can leave behind. The priestess will carry his child alone, while he is content to carry her in his fleeting memory, which he holds in "the middle of [his] being."

In contrast, H.D.'s newly risen woman, full of "this intimate sensing that surpasses analytical understanding," sacrifices her own life so that Jesus may live more comfortably. As a result, what is inside her is "breaking in her head," and feels like what "a lily must feel … at the exact second that the sun pierces its closed leaf." From destruction or death, one begins again; and she is able to assert, finally, "I am Veronica." Innocently but firmly she echoes the divine "I am." From beginning to end, it is Veronica who searches for her real and divine self, emerging from her room/tomb, and discovering her own new life.

By focusing on the final days of Christ, but by writing instead of a Roman woman's personal resurrection, a woman who exhibits, as she says, the "astuteness of a prophetess," H.D. takes on more than Lawrence's arisen messiah. *Pilate's Wife* is attempting to subvert Judeo-Christian culture, which has found few ways to incorporate women into its practice of, or writing about, religion. Yet, the rejected and neglected manuscript of *Pilate's Wife* has represented, until this publication, a continuation of this tragic tradition, which H.D. understood, as early as the twenties and the early thirties. (She had originally intended to write a second novel or more elaborate series of novels, the culmination of which was to be called *Christ in Cyprus*, for which *Pilate's Wife* was supposed to be an introduction.) Fortunately, the rejection of *Pilate's Wife* did not lead H.D. to suppress her revisionist impulses; instead, she became more convinced of her mission to re-create, to resurrect in her poetry the feminine faces of divinity.

Ultimately H.D.'s message of resurrection was to "mount higher/to love," for she equated love with resurrection, claiming that "only love is holy" (*Trilogy*, 114, 122). In terms of religious love, H.D. wished to include the sacred wisdom from all sources, especially that of the forgotten and sacred female self. Surprisingly, though, what H.D. proposes in *Pilate's Wife*, her only full-length biblical novel, is not exclusively woman-centered; in fact, her vision is a collaborative one in which women's faces are remembered, seen next to the faces of men. Essentially—as in so much of the H.D. canon to follow—this early vision posits an ideal of gender harmony, a realigned, sacred partnership through which H.D. speaks to several precursors and contemporaries, D. H. Lawrence among them.

At the the turn of the twentieth century, in *The Varieties of Religious Experience*, William James said the divine was "only such a primal reality as the individual feels impelled to respond to solemnly and gravely, and neither by a curse nor a jest."[13] *Pilate's Wife* concludes, affirming that "primal reality" as Veronica states with conviction, "I am Veronica." In this revisionist novel, her words carry the true countenance of divinity. H.D., writing about *Pilate's Wife* in "H.D. by Delia Alton," said "we, on reading this, have had an answer" to our questions. Part of the answer is realizing that *all* the participants in this quest narrative, including us, are inexplicably drawn toward spiritual investigation, even though each perceives the quest differently and each is at a different stage or depth in the process.

A FEW NOTES ON THE TEXT

In her acceptance speech for the Award of Merit Medal for Poetry, presented by the American Academy of Arts and Letters in New York in May 1960, H.D. thanked the Academy for "measuring in space the whirr of my sometimes overintense and over-stimulated, breathless metres." As editor of *Pilate's Wife*, I have attempted to protect the "whirr" that infuses all of H.D.'s writing, the novels included, with inexplicable but enduring poetic rhythms.

Even though the final typescript of *Pilate's Wife* is marked with over 470 corrections and changes which appear to be in H.D.'s hand, made as she "re-read" in the mid-fifties, a number of details were overlooked. Many involve spelling and punctuation. In order to represent H.D.'s expatriate American/British identity fairly, as well as the hybridized nature of the novel itself, I have maintained the British variants. Other spelling irregularities have been standardized. The matter of punctuation, however, has presented greater challenges. H.D. was an unpredictable self-editor, often diligently correcting the mechanics of dialogue, for instance, in a few chapters and then skipping such a task in others. In cases where her attention was noticeably uneven, I have made decisions based on the obvious need for clarity and the frequency with which she addresses the same or similar details. In her "re-readings," perhaps initiated by the consummate editing and steady influence of Norman Holmes Pearson after World War II, an older H.D. moved tenuously, but moved nonetheless, toward conventional capitalization and punctuation. As a consequence, readers may observe significant differences from her other prose written in the twenties, particularly her more blatantly autobiographical compositions.

Space constraints necessitate hasty but sincere acknowledgments for many who have supported this editing project: Perdita Schaffner, Patricia Willis and the Beinecke Library staff, Peggy Fox at New Directions, Maynard and Florence Mack, Michael Collier and Katherine Branch, Louis Martz, Minda Rae Amiran, Karen Mills-Courts and Patrick Courts, Kimberly Ports, Joe Wittreich, whose vision still inspires, and finally Bob Yandon, my very unselfish husband. A number of grants from the State University at New York, College at Fredonia, have supported research and travel, and I also remain indebted to the Woodrow Wilson National Fellowship Foundation whose award enabled me to read *Pilate's Wife* the first time. Although I have garnered textual assistance from a variety of sources, most generously from my distinguished colleague, Ted Steinberg, who translated and identified the Latin quotations, I take full responsibility for the editing decisions herein.

—*Joan A. Burke*

NOTES

1 Of these five novels, only two were actually published in the 1920s: *Palimpsest* (1926) and *Hedylus* (1928).

2 From the H.D. Papers, Incoming Correspondence, Houghton Mifflin Company (1924–43).

3 Alicia Ostriker, *Feminist Revision and the Bible* (Cambridge: Blackwell, 1993), p. 78.

4 Helene Cixous, "The Laugh of the Medusa," in *The Signs Reader: Women, Gender & Scholarship* (Chicago: Univ. of Chicago Press, 1983), pp. 279–97.

5 Cullen Murphy, "Women and the Bible," in *The Atlantic* 272. (1993), p. 58.

6 Northrop Frye, *The Great Code: The Bible and Literature* (San Diego: Harcourt Brace Jovanovich, 1983), p. 149.

7 Ernst Cassirer, *Language and Myth*, tr. Susanne K. Langer (New York: Dover Publications, 1946), p. 3.

8 Ewa Kuryluk, *Veronica and Her Cloth: History, Symbolism, and Structure of a "True" Image* (Cambridge: Blackwell, 1991), p. 103.

9 According to E.A. Wallis Budge, in Egyptian mythology, Bes is seen as a protector for both mother and child. "… he is often depicted in the form of a dwarf with a huge bearded head, protruding tongue, flat nose, shagging eyebrows and hair, large projecting ears, long but thick arms, and bowed legs; round his body he wears the skin of an animal of the panther tribe, and its tail hangs down and usually touches the ground behind him; on his head he wears a tiara of feathers, which suggests a savage or semi-savage origin." Budge, *The Gods of the Egyptians or Studies in Egyptian Mythology*, Vols. I & II. (New York: Dover Publications, 1969), p. 284.

10 H.D., *Tribute to Freud* (New York: New Directions, 1974), pp. 141–42, 148.

11 Helen Sword, "Orpheus and Eurydice in the Twentieth Century: Lawrence, H.D., and the Poetics of the Turn," *Twentieth Century Literature*, 35 (Winter 1989): pp. 411, 416.

12 *Tribute to Freud*, p. 142.

13 William James, *The Varieties of Religious Experience: A Study in Human Nature*, ed. and introduction by Martin E. Marty (Middlesex: Penguin, 1982), p. 38.

AUTHOR'S NOTE

This theme is no new one.

I began a rough sketch of this story, as early as 1924.

I finished the manuscript, January-February, 1929.

I revised certain sections, July-August, 1934.

The theme of the wounded figure, not dead upon the cross, and its return to life in this life, has fired the imagination of so many that it needs no elucidation. Nor do I claim originality for any of the ideas. I have simply wished to reestablish the familiar scene, in terms of the decadence of the later classical period.

I could not materialise my central figure, Pilate's Wife, under her historical or traditional name, Claudia Procula. However, a Roman lady, of that class, might have had a dozen names, and Veronica might have been one of them.

For historical data, I am particularly indebted to Arthur Weigall, *The Paganism in Our Christianity,* and to Gustave Glotz, *The Aegean Civilization.* I have endeavoured, except for the central motif, to conform to the traditional rendering of the Gospels.

I

NAMES HELD SMALL PART in her consideration, yet she spelled her own arduously, sensing in its hard and pebble-like lustre, some unknown element. She said again, "Veronica, I am Veronica"; that she was the wife of the Roman Governor-General, seated now in pomp below in the outer court-room, held still less sense of probability for her. She said "Veronica," for no apparent reason, while she admonished her servant to be for once, properly attentive, the sandal-strap was too tight, "re-pierce the jeweled thong and later, see to its renewal and, yes, set the knobs of peridot much deeper." Veronica, the wife of the Roman Consul-general, Arch-legate and Vice-governor, so whispering, "Veronica," sensed a hard substance ... blood agate, blood and agate and the rush of water over moss—agate ... Veronica.

"I am Veronica." She could say that and sense it, as if biting it, feeling it. "I can not listen to it," she thought, modifying her elaborate exaggerations. "I can sense it most, feel it like stones, *V-E-R* and *Vera* means true. I am not quite that." Pontius had used her like a lode-stone; he had on various occasions, half-ironically proffered tangled legal matter to her curious brain, for immediate solution. Veronica, of some lost Etruscan forbears, had that astuteness that the mere bred-in-the-bone Roman, at times, lacked somewhat.

Veronica had the astuteness of a pseudo-world prophetess. Pilate used his wife's subtlety, half in pleasure, finding her turn of speech refreshed him; it was avid and pure and without mercy. Justice as Rome fortified it, with scale and manifest weapon, was a monster compound of irreconcilable element, war and peace. In Veronica, one seemed confronted with a compound of like irreconcilable element: purity and voluptuousness, precisely.

Another imperial ambassador, gossip at times had it, would have given the matter swift consideration, turned his powerful yet remorseless hand, palm downward on some marble table, reconsidered it, summoned pomp—and humility in the person of some slave-secretary—had the original writ re-copied and submitted to high authority. Pilate had reason (gossip had it) to so sign away his wife's right to that not inconsiderable title. Yet Pilate's wife remained, in the somewhat straightened high official group in which she moved, still incontrovertibly that. "I am Veronica." That she was, by right and title, the consort of one of Rome's most potent foreign emissaries, did not so much astound her. "I am Veronica" sounded stranger, more irreconcilable than the *domina* and *augusta*, the "my-lady" and "your-highness," echoing about her not too consistent foot-steps. She walked listlessly, at times, in mock solemnity, always a little out of step with the processions she was, by necessity, a part of.

Veronica seemed emotionally, to flutter and evade protestation of too-great friendship, cautiously and diplomatically, like some half-tamed wild-bird. She was wise and pert; a little ridiculously, also like a bird taught to chatter, who senses little if anything of the meaning of the syllables it suitably, or unsuitably, must utter. Wisdom, it has already been well recognized, does not become a woman, save on carved courtroom pedestal or swathed in obliterating garment, seated and forgotten in Vestal solitude; the awkwardness of the prodigy, assimilated and condoned.

A small animal clung, indifferent to the world about it, to a curtain in this lady's bedroom. It was a cat or a marmot or a monkey. No one seemed to know what it was. It was more like an insect, with sudden darting movements, or owl with wings folded over downy feathers. Veronica's room could be measured by this vivid presence, as sometimes, in an over-ornate garden, we make our standard of definition, one industrious giant-bee.

It was a cold room, like its mistress. It had grown up about a personality detached from the glitter surrounding it; so a shell-fish may grow within a shell, so a pearl may cling to the monstrosity of living sea-flesh, its actual progenitor. Veronica cared nothing for this shell; yet it or the monster flesh – Pilate – was, after all, responsible for her life's vivid content. She could measure her years, their success, their failure by these treasures. It was a dead room, or would have been except for the living pulse of this odd creature. It leapt from the curtain now and hunched against a kohl-box on the dressing-table. It was like a soft cocoon, from which a butterfly or a night-moth might wing out.

From the animal, hunched against the kohl-box, to the window-curtain, was considerable distance. Surely, it could not have leapt, it must have flown there. The curtains hung straight, in parallel pleats, as if painted on a wall. Yet those curtains were real, delicate, woven, dyed stuff. When the slightest ripple of breeze caught them, they fluttered inward. Beyond the curtains, was a vision of a winter sun-scape. It was a winter scene but burned and branded in artificial effect of spring—or almost-summer—by the Eastern sunlight.

Painters did not flourish here as in Rome or the porches of the now-effete schools of Athens. The whole landscape seemed to defy their palette. Those late imported rose-peach or rose-apple blossoms were already over, but azaleas from the Caucasian Mountains reproduced their rose and pale-rose tints in formal window-boxes, for which the window was a frame.

There was the inner court, below the balcony. Beyond, across flat roofs, was spread out, a formal city of regular and irregular brickwork, porcelain-tiled roofs and flat expanse of roof-garden; beyond again, were olive-orchards, and those clusters of exaggeratedly precisely-pointed cypresses. The view of the rose-azaleas, of the porch-columns, of the roof-tiles of red or blue porcelain, the regular effect of burnt square-brick wall and geometric road and garden, conveyed nothing to the curious black eyes that were seemingly fixed on the scene, beyond the curtain. The eyes could perceive a midge spinning in the sunlight or could sense, rather than see, the incredible distance from the dressing-table to the curtained window on one side, or on the other, a curtain, about equidistant, that separated this intimate boudoir from the larger, more formal reception-room beyond it. No one knew that those eyes saw almost nothing in the day-light. Its quaint way of staring, without blinking, into the faces of its attendants, had given it a reputation for unusual wisdom. "Oh, Owl of Athens," Fabius, Veronica's favorite centurion of the moment, would address it. Another friend, Memnonius from the lower nome of Egypt, likened it again to Horus.

"Its eyes are hematite," Veronica would cut short discussion, "if you look long enough in them, you will drown."

Perhaps she was speaking truth about herself. She wanted to drown, obviously. She had managed to, but only to come gasping back each time, "disjointed," to use her own word, to the surface of things. "Life and its surface values have to be considered." She had not gotten very far away, with either Fabius Nobilior or Memnonius, from the nome of lower Egypt.

She was not cynical when she said she preferred the animal to these men. She did not consider it even worth while to name Pontius Pilate, along with her other lovers. He was the monster flesh to which her spirit, that pearl, clung really. Had she known it, without him, she would have been lost.

The monkey, evidently, had caught the invisible midge in sun-light. Its black paw shot out like a tongue, then he licked it. It was not quite blind in daylight. Like a cat, it could gauge any distance and prey, near enough at hand, to make clutching worth while. It was a type of beast they had not seen at Rome where small lion-dogs and lions and even leopards had been fashionable. Bright birds, escaped from these same ladies' boudoirs, were often to be seen perched on the olives; they had no claim to that integrant silver background. So this beast. Perhaps its strangeness made the unfamiliar, almost home-like.

A box, a fan, a head-dress flung by hazard on a dressing-table, became real things to Veronica for a moment, in contrast to that beast. It had been brought there to Jerusalem, by some policing vessel, that had spared, from the formidable band of pirates, only this one member. It still held to the manners of its former masters and stole everything.

Aelius Claudius, the particular Prefect of that expedition, had paused with a knife raised, to shudder at the incongruous spectacle of the Owl of Athens, perched on a dead sea-pirate's helmet. He had hastily uttered a prayer as he stared fascinated at the carved smile and mesmeric gaze of this same creature. "The Devil," he said and then laughed. He saw it was not a devil but a moth—anachronism of windless solemn forest, of dark and moist-hot leafage—alighted for some reason, to stress the languor of tropic midnight, in the midst of whip and silver spray of angry winter-water.

This moth-mammal seemed to have brought good luck to Claudius and his expeditions; so that later, when mentioned by his superior for possible preferment, Aelius had diplomatically tendered it to the second steward of the royal household, who, through the usual channels (the usual mix of fate, favouritism, and bribery) had actually brought the creature to the notice of the Palace Prefect. He again seized unexpected opportunity and gained audience with Fabius Nobilior, who, as was openly whispered, had access to the wife of Pontius.

Veronica, clothed for ceremonial, was quaintly touched by the sudden leap which the same animal had made, from the shoulder of Nobilior, onto her purple border. She argued to herself that this was natural, as ceremonial war-gear must be of necessity unsympathetic to such warm and sensitive insectivorous small feet. "Purple," she said, brushing aside obvious flattery, "is more likely the color of his accustomed blossom." Nevertheless, touched by its obvious preference, she treasured the small creature.

It leapt to the inner curtain. The slight scrape of metal on metal told where it had landed. It clung to the dyed stuff, under an embossed ring, which the slightly swaying curtain scraped against the rod running the width of the apartment. Its fore-feet clutched the metal and it drew itself up, to sway like a ridiculous cockatoo. It held itself aloof there, had landed more like a spider on an invisible thread, than a beast jumping.

Veronica's boudoir seemed almost empty in contrast to the room beyond it. The animal ran along the rod, for a few paces. It could not stand upright here, in the space between the rod and the painted ceiling. From the floor beneath, it seemed part of the inverted fantasy of bright leaves, grape-clusters, separate flat-leaves and pattern of pool and summer-house. Veronica had consciously never observed that ceiling, until surprised one day with the intricate beauty of the foreign painting by the sight of her ape, grinning aloft beyond her.

The ceiling was altogether more suitable background for him than the tesselated floor beneath. The floor was littered with low chairs, long settees, various dressing-tables with their several accessories, and separate tables that held each, a single statue or box or image. A chest with carved lid thrown back, showed materials of rare texture and weave; one could guess at hidden treasures. The animal swayed slightly on his curtain-rod, seeming uncertain whether to return to the smaller boudoir, or to jump down on the lid of the chest. Still hesitant, his carved face wore its features, like a mask. His smile seemed to dissemble some eternal and complicated wisdom. Veronica called him Bes, from that least god of the Egyptian hierarchy.

Bes' mesmeric sway was frozen on an instant. His mistress's voice, on the formal side of the dividing curtain, spoke in familiar accent. "Fabius, the thing can be contradicted. Anyway, the only way about it, is to feign—not feign, no—but in god-like tranquility to become indifferent. Indifference is the sign of autocracy, isn't it?" Her companion muttered something. He made toward the inner sanctum where an argument could the more easily, be controverted. But she stopped him. "Here, now, this instant," but he said, "It is of you, Veronica, I am thinking."

She was touched and at the same time, to use her own word, "enervated" by his explicit fervour. "Put your energy into something better. What can the wife of Velleius do, anyway?"

He was not moved by her explicit allusion to an ignoble incident. "This was not, and never did have, any parallel with things here. You don't believe, I suppose, that I care about people; it isn't people. Where would you be, Veronica, without your usual fringes, edges, purple and wide gold? The very badges of nobility could be wrested from your jewel box, by your husband's single trivial gesture. Everything's over, if he lifts a finger."

"O Pontius Pilate—let him—"

"No, no, no—one doesn't jest of these things."

She went back to the beginning, the old familiar argument; she didn't, she repeated, care what people thought. Certainly what they were saying was of no importance to her. "When I am a little, oh the least bit inclined to become enervated by them, I let loose Bes. He climbs up and down, over inaccessible curtains, into sacred chests; pearls and rubies, the very fabulous offerings of this imperial pseudo-gentleman Tiberius, are nothing, I can tell you, to him. Pontificating means nothing to him, flattery means nothing, he wants reality, crumbs of wheat-bread, little cakes of honey, and fruit, peeled and sliced in thin strips. I think then, watching him, that I too am hungry - these words of court favourites, of wan ladies and wearier poets are nothing to me, they're just the pearls and rubies that lie, giving semblance of red and white scattered seeds but are really nothing to one starved, avid (like Bes, like me) seeking sustenance."

"For all your parody of imperial values, Veronica," Fabius answered, "you are the first to grieve and, for all your proud dissemblance, to note side-glances."

She said, "I would be. It is in my nature to be." She called then, unexpectedly, "Bes, Bes," then, lifting her throat, whistled like a bird. Fabius warned her, "I can't argue here where servants, sycophants, boot-licking politicians may enter at any moment." He drew her toward the curtain. Bes dropped like a ripe fruit-pod to the centurion's shoulder.

It had been so for some months, would continue; for how long, none could possibly conjecture. Veronica's liaisons were destined to wither like fruit-blossoms under mid-night hail, in just one soul-searing second; or they endured, summer-flower opening in gradual hieratic secrecy, budding too, giving little shoots and sometimes even flowering (with the smallest intermission, due likely to some diplomatic journey with her husband) as fragrant and as unaccountably fresh, a second season.

Fabius had had difficulty in the beginning; he had rubbed thin over-worn pretensions, but always with a little quirk of eye-brow, a slight over-emphasis of gesture that finally won Veronica. He seemed, like herself, so suitably at one, and yet so entirely separate from the fine scene, they shared. The stage was set as for some later political-social drama of Terence.

While he trod imperial rugs beside her, it held two perfectly
trained and consummate artists, herself and Fabius Nobilior.
The others were ranged in chorus or crowd formation: set en-
trance, exit, the usual formula; inevitable, dreary pause breaking pompous timed greeting to foreign legislator, ambassador
or soldier; the next speech would perhaps be more monotonously insincere, the next pause more pompous, accompanied
this time, perhaps, with gesture. It was "business" of some
subtle order, that held attention, yet must not, under any circumstance, distract from the major action.

Fabius' love-making was that of the polished Roman. He
was courteous to the wife of his superior yet he hinted (with
just as obvious political intention) that he would dare further
—anything (all this was part of the machinery of the moment)
for some more intimate encounter. It had actually surprised
Veronica to find one day that he intended something of the
matter. She had thought it all studied, entirely and beauti-
fully rehearsed; so that when her own little turn came, in this
same boudoir, she had almost given herself away, showing, by
the least possible gesture of astonishment, that she believed
he really loved her. "But that," she had pronounced, "is obviously ridiculous," and she had called the little animal to her,
with the usual click of thumb and finger, and left the matter
to his deeper instinct, or some oracular mood that might
have him fall on her or whisper his message to her.

"Look," she had said, "generalissimo. Do you still like this
creature?" The creature was standing upright. Its breast, thus
displayed, had texture of golden feathers. It rushed to Fabius,
as had been its custom from the first. Fabius stroking its
throat and breast with his forefinger, said "Today it has run
riot in your lilies." "Lilies?" "Hasn't it? Its breast is streaked
with their fire and dusted with their pollen." The remark so

unexpected, so poetical, yet without the usual rhetorical inflection, astonished, then dismayed her. "Fabius. You are a poet." Poetry was at the moment, tiresomely fashionable; Ovid had made it so, Catullus, Propertius, the earlier Mantuan and Horace from Venusia. Fabius answered, "Not in the usual manner." And his kiss, when he sought hers, likewise was not exactly of Augustan precedent. Kisses may fall, unstylized and freshly exquisite, and yet bear the mark of subjection to rote, to rule, to convention, or to bestiality. His bore none of these. Kisses bear marks of former ornament, as coins repeat the heads of King or Victory. His did not. His kiss was as if it was the first he had given, the first she had received. They continued in this manner.

II

From the first, Memnonius had been specifically different.

It was he who suggested these same lilies to shed colour and warmth in the clear water of the basins, sunk for summer-coolness in the court-yard's tiled space beneath her windows. The lilies were part of his consideration for her, along with other adornment, both spiritual and frankly physical. His line of demarcation between those two states, was, he said, so indefinite, that any chance rose, flung by Tiberius' least dancing-girl or boy, might hold the same paradisal nectar, as the very golden lotus of the God or Goddess shining in astral or Ka-form to some prostrate, fasting neophyte.

"Love," said Memnonius from the first nome of lower Egypt, "takes many forms. If," he had specially, logically stated to Veronica, "you know all of them, you will find me an apt pupil. If, as seems possibly not unlikely, I am, in some slight way, your superior, it behooves me, as a very ardent duty, to instruct you."

He had spoken to her at a crowded session, without change of feature, without apparent modification of a voice, that had lately been pronouncing set and formal syllable to Pilate. He had stooped to her fan, which she had deliberately or in sub-conscious panic, let fall. The twin body-servants had stepped forward, figures in a set dance, but Memnonius (centre figure of the same piece) had waved them aside; himself stooping to proffer the instrument, brushed the tip of the spread feathers with lips that but lately, had uttered such logical and peculiar sentiment. His thighs, Veronica noted as he bent, were slight as some Nile serpent. He was altogether boneless, swaying, stepping aside, moving, to her quickened apprehension, like some water-beast in water. He was abstract, logical, literate, illuminated, making no demand on her human sympathy and for that reason, tolerable. She believed he spoke sincerely, when he said, "it behooves me to instruct you."

She endured him later in that his indifference to Pilate removed him from a cycle which had lately tried her. Unlike the usual Asiatic or European legate, he neither concealed nor flaunted the business of his visit. He spoke of it, had done with it, waited response from head-quarters at the Capitol and in the meantime, whiled away hours in apparent happiness.

He neither grumbled at nor patronizingly condoned the provincial circus (as was the custom of most visitors), the theatre and the pleasure-quarter of the city. He was possibly more impressed by this same city than the majority of the members of the bodyguard and the court officials, who passed through Jerusalem on the way to the Far East, or from the East on their return journey to the Capital. Rome? Rome was no more to him than it was to Bes, pawing over rubies and peridot and knobs of turquoise, hoping to find some alluring and tropic red fruit-seed or tiny exotic fruit-pod, there, among them.

Rome offered no spiritual sustenance, Veronica knew, to Memnonius. This the more surprised her, that he should so signally solicit her companionship. "What then," she had said, "do you find in me?"

He had answered, "You have the same eyes. The Nile buds spring from knobs of lustrous fibre, roots of amber, and rise on thin stems toward sun-light. You have not risen."

"You mean you think there is some possibility—you think I might flower differently?"

He said, "No. I think you may wither there, where your bud is curled under, where petals are really curling inward."

She had said, "I have all outer circumstances to prove otherwise."

He said, "Maybe Rome and Egypt stumble toward understanding, speaking awkward dialect."

She said, "I wish there were some trace of awkwardness, of fumbling in your language. I feel horribly near to you. You have no trace of accent. Then when I would pour out myself, I find my way is not your way, you are sombre."

He said, "I don't know what you mean by sombre. I am waiting."

He was waiting, and she believed it, in spite of their physical estrangement. She had pondered long on what he wanted of her. He at least, had no usual Roman lover's care for political appearance. In this, he was unusual. He must care, she thought, at times, about things grander; some such illogical hope held her. Their meetings were of necessity secret, yet without trepidation.

"What must be, must be," he repeatedly asserted. When on occasion, she herself (contrary to her manner with Fabius later) prescribed caution, he replied wryly, "This is written." His "this is written" or "this" somehow forbade further argument. Whether it was a question of a change of head-band or deeper matter, pertaining to their love-rites, his least word fell like clipped stone on marble or like the accompanying exciting rattle of dice in the hands of the inveterate gambler. Veronica, taking hint from him, had full scope of that side of her nature, of which the later Fabius Nobilior disapproved and called *gamin.*

With Memnonius, she was the emotional, social and fatalistic gambler. She learned to play at names and numbers, the names and numbers of stars, and dates of shifting calendars.

On "lucky" days, she would dare unwontedly for "what must be, must be." She also visited new deities in the fashionable manner, and found refuge for the aesthetic side of her nature, in a modernised cult of Isis. The increasing visits of the governor's wife to this shrine, caused no apprehension among the transplanted Romans. At Rome, they had grown tired of the "return to nature," as encouraged by Augustus. The old gods of Latium, so signally re-enshrined, were a bit boorish. In the Capital, a return to the discarded Orientals was in full swing. Some of these gods were modified within reason, took on, here and there, the attributes of the more resilient of the Greeks or the Latin rustics.

In a Rome, where each and every deity was welcome, where the genius of the present emperor and spirit of the Dives must both be propitiated, a lack of interest in some becoming cult—albeit of one's own choosing—might even be misconstrued as dangerously anti-social. A newly imported Isis caused no more apprehension than a newly invented head-band or new way of lacing sandals. Straps, just to the knee or just above the ankle, caused far more discussion and resounding arguments from partisans of both sexes. Lilies? Butterflies? Coronals? Incense? The Greeks had intellectualized, nay, dramatized the least action of the worshiper. Steeped in the Greek cults, the Augustans had turned to their native deities; members of the circle of Tiberius, grown a little worn with prescribed virtue, had also modernized pre-Augustan importations.

Fashions in thought partook of new pleats, as folds in

dresses, head-bands worn jewelled this side or that, wide or narrow, high or low, upon imperious forehead. Sandals and soft boots and sandal-straps differed succeeding winters. So religions. Isis wore straight pleats, her hair was dressed low on the neck; with a slight change of garment-fold or head-dress, she might be an exotic Ionian or even an Etruscan. Veronica propounded this matter to Memnonius, who seemed to take it seriously.

"No," he said, "she couldn't be Etruscan. Your Etruscan hierarchy is a Greek hierarchy of marble and snow, turned into luminous and murderous metal. Steel is in their faces, in their cruel smiles, in their inevitable utility. Useful? Yes, I consider the Etruscan, for all his claim to fabulous antiquity and his somewhat smug self-sufficiency, a sort of transplanted—well, Jew almost. He is viperish and dark. His reality has never been revealed, save in the egoistic smile of the Hellenic sun-god, modified to steel, to lascivious cruelty. The Greek was cruel, lascivious. But never the two together."

She interrupted, "You consider Etruscans vipers?"

"Yes, with more sting than wisdom."

She said, "Thank you," and yet secretly was flattered, "But your Isis. Certainly, she is only an earlier Aphrodite?"

He said, "No, you are completely misled. The cult of Aphrodite is the cult of the recognisable; at her most luminous shrines, a goddess, true, of poetry, inspiration, but always sustained in open language. The whole interest in Isis—" He paused. "Well, it was only the dead held her."

Veronica waited for Memnonius to continue, found him, in her own phrase, sombre. "She must have had other lovers."

As his smile flashed back at her, Veronica realized he had rallied from "sombreness" to artificiality. She had known he would. Well, if he would not expound the secret doctrine, why hint so at it? *Was* there a secret doctrine? Memnonius, in his usual manner, hinted dolefully or with mock humour at "inner mysteries," but unlike other Egyptians of her acquaintance, his hints seemed more than at the usual obvious, Oriental duality.

With Memnonius, there seemed always to be a door about to be flung open, a hand reaching and then as swiftly withdrawing.

Veronica said, "Isis *did* go clothed like Aphrodite, in blue, in sea-purple."

"Not sea-purple; if you must, sky purple."

"Is the sky ever purple?"

"In lower Egypt, the sun, low-lying, sheds beams like a great star. Such sun-light, Isis knew, was the "love-soul" of her Master, Osiris, rising, dying; dying, to be awakened. Each day he rose, each day he died. She knew the body of the god, her earthly consort, waited elsewhere for her. How could she have other lovers?"

Veronica answered, "The whole argument of the faith has no foundation in reality." His quick eyes caught hers. Then he smiled again, his usual Memnonius-smile, set, artificial, "O, possibly?"

"They say she remained a Virgin."

"Why not?"

Veronica did not know if he was mocking. She would find out.

"How could Isis, the mother of Horus, remain virgin?"

"Virginity is an attribute of divinity. God alone—Ra, the supreme Diviner—can say this Goddess, this Woman, this wild-dove, is a virgin. God being all-powerful can decree anything."

Again she caught him up with "and what about the mutilation and hideous disfigurement of his own Son? I can never really conceive how so sensitive a race as yours, can still accept the possibility of omniscient and beneficent Deity, mutilating the helpless body of his Child."

She paused waiting; then, "I can perhaps understand the worship of such mutilation. Men were ever cruel—and curious. They stand gaping at a body, crushed by accident by a passing cart-wheel, or at full-blooded animals, writhing under blunt instruments of slaughter, as if nothing else could ever distract them from such fascinating spectacle. Nothing delights man more than hideous slaughter and disfigurement, whether of man or beast. Say what you will—that there is subtle and philosophic reasoning on the part of the priesthood, who actually defined this manner of worship; that even in its most exaggerated form, men actually kneel, beseeching such mutilated images of slain gods—but is there, is there any logic in saying that *God* actually did it?"

She again paused, wondering why he did not answer, then gained her breath to ardently continue.

"Admit that the slaughtered, or foully mutilated, body of a Hero or God has to be set before people, who have so little conception of beauty or life that they must worship, even kneel before it. Say that must be. But how can any enlightened people say *God not only permitted, but decreed it?*"

Veronica was astonished at her unwonted passion. Memnonius was right. The cult of Isis, for all her apparent indifference, save for the mere husk or shell of it, had yet flamed her imagination, as no other conventional state-festival of the Roman Venus, or no other literary Greek parallel, had ever done. Even their old Goddess of Etruria, had not touched her thus—with all the careful array of pomegranate, cones and gilded fretwork of pear-shaped bud and half-opened blossom. She had always felt something of the spirit of that stylized Etruscan—a version of some earlier Ionian Cyprus—had passed into her, that day when she and her brothers, children of some eight and ten and twelve years, had collected the native servants and protected the small, disused shrine from mutilation by their father's new wife and her strange Campanian servants.

These Campanians could not see beauty in the tortured lascivious mouth of the same thin Goddess. She had afterwards been stowed away somewhere—safe. Where?

Veronica had never quite forgotten her; the memory of that image had returned with startling clarity, just now, when she had said to Memnonius that this Isis was like another. She recognized uncanny similarity in the two images, but to be fair, she had to admit there was yet some even more curious difference. What was it that their cruel, thin, tortured, little Goddess lacked? Isis was faithful—was just that the difference?

Isis was a magician and goddess of wisdom. The Greeks, for all their immense pragmatism and logic, had had to split their image of the perfect Woman in two: Love, faithless, and Wisdom, loveless. Yet even Aphrodite and Athené, re-modelled—flung into some blasting furnace, to return, one perfectly welded figure—would yet lack something, something of the magic that Isis held in Egypt. The sun rising, the sun setting, perhaps held different values to different people. She said, "Osiris, giving all blessing to man, was yet defeated. Surely, the Greeks are more logical. Their sun-god had power and did not disdain to use it. Beauty must be protected." Veronica felt the ardour of her statement breaking through her, like a very visible aura.

She wondered at her own astuteness and her religious definition. She felt herself suddenly lost, baffled by Memnonius' silence. She had to concentrate those odd, unseeing eyes of hers, squint almost, into his curious features. There was, what she called that "Memnonius-smile," eternal, carved like that of her own Bes, far too old and wise to be in any way intrigued by any facile logic. He rather pointedly evaded further argument and, as if in recognition of an intellectual discourtesy, became unduly tender, likening Veronica again to a Nile flower, infolded. He wanted, he said, these flowers to remind her of herself, of the Goddess, Isis.

There were red ones, purple ones, like inner petals of pomegranate blossom, white, rose-white and yellow. She had chosen the yellow, perhaps unconsciously thinking of the sun-rays of Osiris. On further occasion, when she again sought argument on the subject of the obscure mystery, he had answered, "You have only to watch your lilies."

Veronica had continued to meet him furtively and retained exquisite memory of their converse. "The goddess will protect us," he had asserted when she, as her habit then was, had spoken of possible censure. His "what must be, must be" and her own well-recognized habit of visiting outlying, foreign shrines had given them sufficient excuse for meeting. Veronica could not say when he began to tire her. With exquisite tact however, he continued sending or bringing her fresh bulbs and roots, wrapped in palm-leaves, so that at each and every season, she might have the gold lily-heads, floating wide open or folded, like lumps of opaque jasper or green Nubian beryl—to remind her of Memnonius, of Osiris and his improbable father, who had, with all power of divinity, permitted mutilation of the body of the man-God.

The last time she had asked him of this, he had feigned forgetfulness of all their former converse.

"You forget," Memnonius had curtly answered, as if this must settle further argument, "the more intimate parentage. Geb and Nut, heaven and earth, were the immediate parents of the gentleman in question," and she was still further baffled (was he always laughing at her?). "Ra was only his grandfather."

III

It was Memnonius who suggested that she go to Mnevis.

She said, "And who is Mnevis?" She corrected herself. "Or, should I say, 'what is Mnevis?'"

He said "It's a new prescription."

"O," she said, "I thought as much. It sounded like a honey and cream compound a Sicilian, I once knew, used for blotting out moles."

He said, "It's for psychic blots, however, not mere physical."

She said, "Can't you, for once, keep the two, Memnonius, separate?"

He said, "The two are never separate."

They were quibbling, they both knew. Veronica came back like an agile gambler, it was her throw. "But anyhow, this Mnevis?"

He said, "I happen to be serious."

She said, "How can you be? To say 'Mnevis' purses the lips and tongue, like a snake hissing."

He said again, remembering talk of the Etruscan serpent, "With more hiss than wisdom." He did not mean that.

She said, "Well, then, who is it?"

He said, "There's a girl, I think she's from Crete. I don't know how she got there or how she ended up here."

"Is there anything astonishing about that? There are so many girls, back and forth, like flotsam and jetsam, washed inward from the sea-coast."

"She isn't," he said, "flotsam,"—he pronounced the little-used word, strangely—"nor yet jetsam."

"Do you know what those words mean?"

"Certainly, *augustissima*."

"Well, what is this lotion?"

He ignored her question.

"I am superstitious," he said, "there must be something in it."

"In what, Memnonius?"

"In this. She bears the name—that is, her somewhat out-landish Cretan name, *sounds* like the syllables they pronounce in the old cult at Heliopolis. It is the name of that local Apis or that bull-Osiris." He didn't know, he added, if she came from that same city, or even if her name, spelt out in Greek, or even bastard Crete and Latin, would actually be Mnevis. As she pronounced her odd name, it had sounded like that of the bull-God, and this had strangely roused him. He was forever following threads that led to nothing. He said as much, "I am always following clues that seem to lead nowhere. This time, I stand on the edge of the precipice."

"And you want me to jump off for you?"

"Well, not exactly that, Veronica; you might turn out another Ariadne."

She was tired of playing at being so many people, she said. However, she might possibly try this, later. She would think about it. He said, she would not regret it and added, he had an ulterior motive, frankly. She did not ask him what that was. She was certain it was nothing ordinary; not any sort of thing that she could guess at. He would tell her, if he chose; if he did not, no amount of teasing, nor patient ingenuity, could get an answer from him. He would tell her what he chose to.

He did condescend to explain that the girl was a sort of

fortune-teller. Veronica had guessed that much. When she said she was tired of ordinary professionals, whose eyes were always half aware of palm-marking, and half aware of gold or purple border, he said, "Mnevis is not like that. You are not to go in any sort of border."

"How am I to go then? Don't they gauge the future, by what sort of ear-rings you wear?"

"You are not to wear any ear-rings—perhaps for fun, some paste ones."

She said, "That would not be fun."

Well, she must wear some sort of disguise, dress up for the show. She was accustomed to playing at being someone else, while knowing all the time that the wife of Pilate was adequately protected. Her seemingly secret visits to old shrines, were all reported. Memnonius really wanted her to go incognito, this time. He had thought out a rôle for her. She was to be the second sempstress-assistant, the one he had once passed, in the outer corridor, on the way to her mistress's boudoir.

"But that girl has red hands."

"That doesn't matter. You have got to be something simple."

"She isn't—" But something made her stop quibbling. Memnonius was really serious.

Mnevis had, he told her, a new method of tabulating fortunes, playing as it were, one game with several sets of pieces. Where one would not answer, another was brought into action and the first probably, "out of pique," as Memnonius put it, "would come round." Mnevis, it appeared, check-mated one's stars with places, one's names with numbers, future events with past events, and present probability with the chart of past endeavour. Veronica was not impressed. She said again that she was tired of being favoured with dull rote, with sing-song, all intensely boring and illiterate. The eyes of these professional fortune-tellers were always half aware, she repeated, of palm markings, and half aware of gold or purple border.

The next time he saw her, he asked how she found Mnevis. She said, she hadn't been yet; she knew that he knew this, but as he seemed to expect an answer, she gave him one. They had both met, after a particularly suffocating assembly, in one of the half-private ante-rooms; they passed formal remarks about the weather, for the benefit of a group of delegates; when they left, their eyes met, half in wonder that this chance meeting, meant now, just nothing to them. Their half-poignant, half-ironical, unspoken words seemed to be, "There was a time when—." The very fact that there had been a time when such a meeting might have meant more than the world to them, in some way, still subtly bound them. They were not excited, certainly. Yet old habit caused Veronica to take stock of the room before she leaned forward to Memnonius' whisper: "you _must_ go, the woman has converse with enchanters, new sorts of magic."

Veronica had decided, after their last discussion, that the subject of the woman frankly bored her. She had decided not to go. But Memnonius had come back to his tiresome Heliopolis.

"Her eyes have the same sort of pupils as Veronica's, those dilated half-eyes of the psychic-gifted." His own then met hers, but they did not match his set grin.

She ignored the matter of eyes altogether, and repeated

that she was tired of fortune-tellers, who only told her one thing. They invariably said she would have a letter from across the water, and she inevitably did; it was always the old steward on her deceased brother's Etruscan farmland, dunning her for money which she (during a crisis earlier, in the Capital) had borrowed without her husband's knowledge. "You know, Memnonius, these little extraneous bills that husbands frown at."

There was suspicion, she thought, as of kohl under those eye lids. His eyes shocked her. She had only now, just noticed that dark-smudged under-rim. Was it possible Memnonius was as tired as that, as ill? "Have your eyes looked like that, always?"

He opened them wide, and instantly she could have sworn that other eyes were set there—plunder of temple-statue, onyx, dark hematite, black crystal. Images might fuse and form there; she looked into shaft of buried temenos, there might be chanting, shaking of mysterious amulets, Ankh, the Stairs or Uzat.

She said, "Is it Ankh, the Stairs or Uzat?" but he did not seem to hear her, and she found herself gazing into those dark eyes that were flecked with inverted pin-points, the eyes of Memnonius, from the lower nome of Egypt.

Veronica finally went to Mnevis, partly out of curiosity, partly to tease Fabius Nobilior, who disapproved of these excursions.

She sat in the chair she supposed all the clients sat in. Yes, I suppose, she thought, I am a client. She looked round a room that was empty, yet seemed charged with implication—as a temple-cella derives intensity from one small statue set upright, on an altar. There were things in the room, surely? It wasn't, by any means, empty; her eyes swept, right, left. She had been set down by her bearers a short street distant, and she thought her disguise perfect (it would have been difficult to convince her that just that set of head would give her away, anywhere). She thought she was protected.

Well, as far as Mnevis was concerned, she was; the woman, it was obvious didn't care in the least, who she was. Veronica remembered that she was supposed to be that sempstress—that extra girl, from some outlandish mart—the only one who could re-weave a bit of heirloom or court-decoration that couldn't be discarded. She had said to Memnonius that the girl's hands were red and she sensed her own, lying in her lap. She had slipped off the heavy official signet that Pilate insisted she wear on these occasions. Her hands were cold. The woman would probably ask to see them. She did not realise her hands; how beautiful they were. They were, perhaps, the one flawless thing about her. Her chin, when one stopped to regard her, was a little over-shot and her forehead too high. Her shoulders were compact, a little hunched forward; she moved self-consciously, somewhat lacking the arrogance that passes for autocracy; she was accused, at times, of being awkward. Her feet were as lovely as her hands, set forward, placed before her, like the seated Isis. She was the seated Isis.

None of this escaped the girl Mnevis.

She began at once.

Would Madame care to sit nearer to the window? Would Madame prefer to recline on this couch? (The girl was seated on a divan. She rose.) Would Madame be happier if her servant might be permitted to loosen the clasp, at the throat of

her cloak? She said "Madame" and "Her servant," but she
didn't mean it, Veronica thought; her tone was slightly acrid.
She is impertinent. "Would Madame allow—"

"Sit down. I suppose—our friend—" (did she actually know
his name?) "informed you I was coming?"

Mnevis sat down.

"Yes, Madame."

"Why do you call me Madame?"

"It is customary with the clients. I do not actually know
your Ladyship's several titles."

"I didn't mean that. Why do you say, your Ladyship?"

"It is the custom—"

"I don't mean that either. I mean, you know—surely you
were informed—I am a mere—I am a sort of work-woman for
someone of importance."

"You were never a work-woman."

"Why do you say that?"

"The hands of work-women—"

"O, the hands. It is needed in my business." (Should she
turn herself now, into a masseuse or a hairdresser? She supposed it was too late.)

"Would her Ladyship show her servant, her hands?"

"O—"

"Straight out."

"You have the mystic-cross, somewhat starkly outlined, between the line of heart and the head-line. Further, you have
the slightest tracing of a Ring of Solomon upon the mount of
Jupiter. You run contrary to reason, your heart is not altogether assured of your own values. Your mind, dominated by

the mystic-cross rooted at the base of the head-line, disqual-ifies you for deep and real enjoyment. The mount of Venus is low, the fate-line is broken. Where the fate-line rises toward the line of Apollo, there is another branch, towards Saturn. Art that should enthrall you, is again nullified by religious speculation."

But what was all this? The words were intoned; Mnevis almost seemed a priest, before an altar. Veronica found herself losing her sense of identity. Who am I? Why, I am Veronica: or am I Veronica? What is it, the girl's saying? She said something about the mount of Venus, used that Capitoline *cliché;* any beggar in the Forum could have told her that much. She was no better than the gypsy that had crept on her, unawares, once when she was alone with—with? Was it Pilate? It happened a long time ago, before she came here. Where am I? Why, this is a suburb of Jerusalem, I came here in my litter. Fabius insisted that I have his escort, but I told him Pilate had other plans for my afternoon. What of Fabius? It was Memnonius who sent me.

"O yes—the mount of Venus."

"You are not really, Madame, interested in the mount of Venus."

The girl had returned to "Madame."

Veronica jerked back to the room and the room's contents. She would come back, be the wife of Pilate. "O, yes. You wrong yourself and you wrong me. You guessed my object exactly."

"Madame didn't come here to learn about a lover. All that, she knows already—" Veronica made an almost unconscious gesture, as toward a waiting guard. But she as swiftly, recol-lected. She was not in her own palace, and she was not supposed to be herself. Memnonius had especially asked her to retain some form of anonymity. Memnonius had succeeded in making her feel important. What was it that he wanted? He had specifically wanted something. And after all, why should the girl not say that? It was not really an impertinence, it was only that the words came strangely. They were not common women discussing their various gladiatorial preferences, they were–they were–something different. Yes, Memnonius was right. They were somehow related.

"The–the *friend*, who sent me to see you, noted that we have the same eyes." Veronica used her own deliberately. She noted again that the little room held specific trophies.

There was an incised plaque, traced with odd letters or symbols, hanging above a low table, upon which were set two candles. One wide lily floated in a flat bowl. There was a cross above the door, carved with hieroglyph or symbols of some Asiatic creed or cult. The woman went on talking.

Veronica's eyes came back to that dark head, bent, so enthralled, gauging line and cross-line, as if deciphering some fabulous papyrus. She thrust out words–definitive words of Mnevis.

"I will later tell you your numbers. If I may predict, Mercury, whom the Greeks call Hermes, will have some strange counter-influence. Here, where Venus is barred, there is sign of strength in some other region."

The cross held Veronica's attention. She had not seen one of just this peculiar attribute. Such a cross, she had heard, had been stamped upon foreheads. Some native prophet, she believed (Ezekiel?) had had them stamped upon the foreheads of a chosen people, just as such crosses were branded across the flanks of pasturing cattle. This idea, at once, fascinated her; she had never traced the story.

"What is that cross?" The woman looked up. Veronica perceived eyes, filled with pupils. Did her own look like that? Memnonius had said, "those blotted-out half-eyes of the psychic-gifted." The phrase hadn't sounded quite right. Memnonius so seldom misused the Latin idiom—psychic-gifted? It seemed for the first time, that she had caught him (to use his own phrase), "speaking awkward dialect."

"—our—friend, said you had the strange blotted-out half-eyes of the psychic-gifted."

"Madame isn't in the mood for the reading?"

"Yes," Veronica assured her, "she feels just like it." She spoke blithely now, as one accustomed to display a metallic glitter before inferiors, trying fitters who, out of revenge, keep ladies standing beforehand, in anticipation of inevitable, tedious, extra tasks imposed upon them. There was always that class-duel. "How long will she stand?" and "She shan't know how much she has annoyed me." "I must have the drapery just right, Madame," and "O, no, how could I be tired?"

This appeared to be some sort of petty intellectual daring and defiance of the same order. Veronica could never take anything quite simply, nor recognize any sort of possibility of spontaneous friendship. She could not realise that Mnevis was startled at her palm-marking, and wanted to befriend her. She couldn't remember that Memnonius had told her that she, her very self—Veronica—was actually an inferior dress-maker of the inner circles; Veronica's disproportionate dignity had not impressed Mnevis, who knelt now under the strange cross, searching a square box for ink and brush and paper.

"I must tell you, you must not be discouraged."

"I? How have I been discouraged?"

"Your years, the lines, the numbers–" Mnevis spread out the page and inked in detail of letters and stars and numbers, "–point to one thing. A complete change: spiritual, emotional, physical, what you will."

"Change? We are always changing."

"I don't mean travel or change of outer circumstance, though that is here too. Mercury, whom the Greeks call Hermes, is here with you. Here Mercury has a double value. It would be better for you, having the mystic-cross so singularly attached to the head, rather than the heart-line, to consider Mercury. But to consider him perhaps, more in his early character. He is, of course, Thoth of the Egyptians." Mnevis had marked a cross, the T-Cross with long upright and bar, set across the top, like that same letter.

"You must consider this cross among your attributes. It is transformed, in the staff of Hermes; the cross-bar becomes the heads of the serpents, wisdom of heaven and earth, what Memnonius calls 'up and down stairs.'" Mnevis smiled faintly, at the mention of Memnonius. So the girl knew him by his name, and knew that he had sent her.

"You–like him?"

"Memnonius?" For the first time, those odd, un-seeing eyes looked straight at Veronica. "*Like* Memnonius?" Mnevis laughed. Her words seemed impertinent and Veronica felt herself stiffen with class-consciousness.

"Well–yes, unless 'like' is too informal an expression. I judged he had done much for you."

Mnevis answered astonishingly, "He has done nothing for me."

She went on, "What can anyone do for anyone?" It seemed again, an improper thing to say, for an inferior. Was she an inferior? What was she?

"Well—position, advancement. Surely, you depend for patronage on the recommendation of one client to another."

"The clients, as you call them, are so many midges dancing in a bright, or dull sun. One can focus, direct, draw the line of the sun-ray, show each midge the line of his sun-pattern."

"The line of—?"

"His sun-ray or pattern. One can say to this one, go on in the darkness, it leads straight to the light, one can say to this one, you are spinning joyously above a pit of destruction, one can disseminate a little of this wisdom as a flower its honey—"

"A flower—its—"

"*Sweeter than honey in the honey-comb, moreover by this is thy servant warned*—by this and by this and by this."

But Veronica wasn't put off by glibly quoted precepts. "What right, anyway, have you to speak lightly of one in so exalted a position?"

"I can't see that Memnonius is exalted. He comes here when he's tired out."

"Don't you know who the—the—patrons are, he sends you?"

"No. It is specifically arranged beforehand that they come in odd disguises. He sent in a cheese-monger's widow, one day, who perfectly aped refinement. He says, most souls long after disguise of some sort—disguise of soul or body. And he says, I can judge better, if they throw off their usual habits. The people who come here, don't as a rule come for—for frivolous purposes."

"What then, do they come for?" Veronica knew that all this was simply quibbling. The séance was at an end but she didn't want to dart too swiftly from the comfort of this half-

light into the rabble outside. The girl had gone on, talking on two separate levels; so had Veronica. She must get herself (this strange parody of an actress) into her waiting litter.

She knew there was no answer to her question, nor did Mnevis pretend to answer. She said simply, "Suggesting happiness, toward faith, upholds the saddest creatures. I judged you had come like the rest, out of sadness."

"No," said Veronica, "out of satiety."

IV

VERONICA INSISTED, "You are quite wrong, Fabius, the woman is a scholar." Fabius was accustomed to Veronica, in a perverse mood; he could cope with that. It was her unwonted credulity that annoyed him. He could hardly object to Veronica's making one visit out of curiosity, to this gypsy; it was her repeating the experience that upset him. How many times had she been, with or without his knowledge? He didn't dare to ask her.

He said, "Scholar? What do you mean by scholar?"

"She has studied Assyrian charts, the names of stars and star-clusters, has watched the skies, has risked her life, hidden behind curtains at assemblies to hear what the elders proffer. She has made a business of knowledge, as some women make a pastime of love."

"A pastime of love? I thought that *was* her past time."

"Not her pastime—occasional interlude. She was a singing-girl, a professional sort of singer."

Fabius was not impressed with singing-girls, moreover he found the phrase, "hidden behind curtains at assemblies," curiously oppressive. "There's positive danger, Veronica, mixing yourself up with that sort."

Veronica answered, "She isn't."

Fabius said, "Isn't what?"

Veronica said, "That sort."

Fabius repeated himself, "I thought you told me she was a sort of prostitute," which occasioned repetition again on her side, "I told you she was a professional sort of singer. I said she sang—folk-songs, songs of her own people."

"How can that make a difference? A woman appears in wine-cellars and low houses, singing."

"Her songs are songs of the tulip-flowers in blossom and a god, native to those flower-fields like Adonis, but called, I am told, Asterios."

Fabius was equally indifferent to Adonis and Asterios. He answered, "There are thousands of Asiatic singing-girls in Rome and in Rome's cities."

"Jerusalem, is hardly Rome's city, is it?"

"I say, there are thousands of these girls—exactly of one mind."

"What mind, Nobilior?"

"Grasping, cringing, commercialism of those classes."

"She asked nothing for the somewhat elaborate chart of my stars, numbers, or the lines of my palm. I have consulted many of those so-called minor prophets—she didn't prophesy. She made a chart, logically predicted." Fabius was not impressed. "She is some sort of spy of that Egyptian—" His thought had returned to *hidden behind curtains.*

Having got round to Memnonius, Veronica dropped the subject, for a moment. But she came back to it.

"She made me see the fields—she isn't Asiatic."

"You chatter to-day like a mad creature—what *is* the matter with you?" It is true that the eyes of Veronica were flecked with odd light; colour came to her rather gaunt high cheek-bones.

"Nothing's the matter with me, Fabius. But this Egyptian or Greek Mnevis—what is Crete, anyway?—seems to have given me ideas—ideals—"

"Of what sort?"

"Pictures rather than music—I mean, the fields, she says, in Crete, are alive with tulips. She isn't really an Egyptian. Her name itself, Mnevis, is a sort of Latinized version of Greek or Cretan, having something to do with the ceremonial of the first gathering of wild-tulips. Memnonius linked her up, for some reason of his own, with Heliopolis."

"Heliopolis, Persepolis, Sardinopolis, what's that to me, Veronica?" Fabius was tired. He had consented against his better judgment, to undertake a tactful sort of diplomatic mission having to do with the returned Eastern soldiers. He had found his task exceptionally trying.

He had been asked to verify that certain rites, having to do with a cult of Mithra, were now alarmingly prevalent among the returned legionaries. He considered tendering spiritual advice or criticism to common soldiers, a duty quite outside the province of an "officer and a gentleman." That Veronica should have chosen this particular day, to put forward the creed and beliefs of a half-caste Cretan dance-girl, particularly annoyed him. The fine fibre of Augustan precedent, he was continually reminded, was being eaten into by a kind of virus. Here, there, wherever you looked, men and women of fashion were seeking psychic stimulus. He considered it unhealthy.

"*Sparge rosas,*" he whispered only just in time. Veronica drew nearer. "Yes—that's it. Haven't we?" "Haven't we?" "Scattered, I mean, our roses."

The Horatian syllable, thrown out half in jest—a subtle sort of invitation—was not received, as was customary, by Veronica. It was her habit to reply with swift Alexandrian, or early Greek metre: a ball tossed, to be caught and returned as swiftly. Veronica neither caught it nor returned it. It seemed to fall, metallic in its clatter, among the silver vases, the incised upright ornaments, carved with Augustan oak-leaf and derivative wild-laurel.

To Veronica, this subtle under-play was not likely to pass unnoticed. She thought, "Our minds are crowded with ornate syllables as this room is with drear and obvious ornaments." It had been easy in the past, to answer Horatian or Vergilian syllables with Homeric ones, and to be lost, suddenly, in a world of rivers, stately pines or fragrant cedars.

Greek syllable, to her mind, was flexible like harp-strings. She thought this, saying nothing to Nobilior; *sparge rosas* was heavy, it was obvious.

Her eyes, Nobilior noted, were wide, drowned with exaggerated pupil. This, he seldom saw, had in fact, now he considered it, known only in moments of intense intimacy—drugged, great, exaggerated eyes staring fixed, cataleptic.

"I never see you look like this—except—I mean, why are your eyes drowned out now, in blackness?" The sun was pouring through half-parted curtains. That, too, was contrary to custom. Veronica usually drew away in shadow, sometimes she was almost invisible; a gleam of bracelet or odd jewel like moonlight among dark trees, showed she was there.

"I never recall your facing me in sunlight—not actually in sunlight. Our own terrain was different." Veronica knew what he meant, when he said briefly, "Our own terrain."

She thought, "I see that I have tired him," but it wasn't, she knew, quite that. "Nobilior, I have bored you."

He rose. "Surely, Veronica, you would only trouble to invent such an elaborate lie, to cover over my own ineptitude." He was standing by the curtain. "No, Fabius." The small creature, Bes, had leapt as usual, from some hidden corner, was pushing its blunt face into the centurion's shoulder. "No, Fabius." She didn't know, for the moment, where she stood. Dazed with a sudden pre-vision of inner splendour, she had found that her outer kingdom and her inner sanctity had some link missing. She did not want to lose Nobilior.

Would Memnonius understand this? Yes, she needed Fabius Nobilior. "No—sit here—sit closer, Fabius. This woman, speaking as she did of time and of values out of all Roman computation, set something, somewhere, glowing."

"This—woman? Then Veronica it *was* this woman?"

"O, Fabius, why waste time or words? Yes, I told you; she was called for something, meaning wild-flower, the wild-tulip. She spoke of the Cretan god as a—Greek might speak of dead Adonis. But to her, he was not dead, he was living simply. She has known someone, who conceivably might have—been him."

Fabius seated beside Veronica, with the small animal nosing along the bronze of his fore-arm, seemed to hear echo of some flute-note. He had heard this himself, somewhere—where? Lately, he had heard just such talk of the re-adjustment of the dead and living.

"*Veronica—*" The small animal had fallen from the bronze arm of the centurion and was playing with the tasselled girdle-end that, as he pawed it, tap-tapped on the marble pavement.

"—I remember."

"Remember?"

"Your eyes—they reminded me of something. It was the tiresome task of Aelius Claudius."

"Claudius?"

"Have you forgotten Claudius? He obtained disproportionate favour with authority because you, my Veronica, once

deigned to smile upon him. Don't you remember? A somewhat tiresome and alert young general (at least, he is now)
who took triremes, slew barbarians, stained the Mediter-
ranean a peculiar scarlet."

"Claudius?"

"Then capturing a singular sort of daemon, he made a
present of it to—Veronica."

"A daemon? Claudius?" She remembered then. "Claudius.
Yes—it was he brought Bes to me. I *do* remember Claudius."

"Veronica, I, too, have had peculiar intuition."

"Intuition?"

"I was sent by this same wretch, Claudius, who didn't want
the tricky business of enquiring into this new Mithraism, the
religion of the cohorts." Veronica raised a warning hand,
drawing the small beast to her. The curtains parted. Continu-
ing as it were the same conversation, in the same voice, yet
turning from Veronica, Nobilior said to Pilate, "My men kept
me."

The two Romans spoke formally, neither over-conscious of
the presence of Veronica, nor specifically ignoring it. In fact,
they turned toward her, from time to time, as if for judgment
or corroboration of the affair in hand. Pilate had been wont
to assume this attitude toward Veronica, in all official circles;
his subordinates, naturally took colour from him. Nor was it
strange to have found Nobilior here. Pilate used Veronica's
rooms on occasions of informal conference. There was no
cause for awkwardness.

Veronica held the little beast in the curve of her arm;
Fabius stood easily yet on guard, before the high official;

Pilate himself had the dignified yet somewhat heavy bearing of some Capitoline general. Pilate continued, half-facing his wife, in conference with Nobilior.

"I mean, Fabius, the matter of the caverns leads, or may lead, to secrecy. I wish you would investigate it further." Fabius assured his master that the secret cult of the new Eastern Mithra was only a development of a more ancient one, quite harmless, a sort of Zoroastrianism, an intellectualized sun-worship, having nothing whatever to do with any sort of rebellion. "In fact, otherwise."

Pontius Pilate answered, "Religion and rebellion go hand in hand. Let these men sacrifice as is customary, to the effigy of Caesar." Fabius assured Pilate that that matter, so often discussed between them, did for shop-keepers and the lesser merchant populace.

"You can not command a soldier, in matters of religion. Superstition is part of every soldier's outfit and equipment. How could men fight, die indifferently, were it otherwise?" Fabius Nobilior stated specifically, that mere superficial civic sacrifice—outer semblance of devotion to the emperor's image—was just as much a part of the badge of service as a man's helmet or his colours. But that was different, public.

"Having made that public gesture, surely these men, back from the Far East and perilous campaign, should not be bothered in their inner private worship."

Pilate said he had no rigid objection to any particular cult; it was these caves, he found displeasing. It was obvious that secret caverns, meeting places for sacrifice and communion (fast spreading among the soldiers) might be neat pasture later, for the sowing of seeds of active rebellion in the provinces.

"What," Pilate forensically demanded, "am I here for?"

Fabius said it was well known, in official circles, that Pilate had his hand tightly on the reins of all the provinces. "You were put here for a reason."

Pilate knew the reason. Veronica was not listening. At a sign from Pilate, Fabius pronounced the usual sonorous "Vale," with appropriate gesture.

Pilate said, "No. I have affairs below," and he left them.

Veronica said, "What is this new religion?"

"I was just about to tell you before Pilate entered," Fabius said, "Mithraism. A star was seen in the East and shepherds, in the Aryan mountains, saw a host of angels descending. There was pronouncement of benediction and Mithra was born, son of light. The darkness is the evil spirit, and goodness is the god, Mithra, light. These men have introduced no new startling doctrine; they concern themselves simply with the eternal balance of wickedness, beneficence; the day, the night; light, darkness."

Veronica said, "Yes. But how can this abstract imagery help common soldiers, who crave outward image as a rule? The untutored want Victory upon a standard, Vesta by the hearth-fire, Mercury in the counting-house, Apollo by the gate-way."

Fabius was seated again, beside her. His fingers were busy untangling the web Bes had made of the fringed end of Veronica's girdle. He spoke with head bowed, his hardy yet fine hands magnanimously engaged in the task of straightening it out. Nobilior spoke this time, simply, with no ornament of Augustan metre.

"What good is Mercury in the Scythian desert? Does Capitoline Jupiter answer, on the peaks of the Dalmatian mountains? Has fastidious Venus been known to enter the lowly and malsaine dens of the low drinking-houses? There is one god, always approachable in Scythia, in Syrio-Phoenicia, in the Bactrian marshes. There is one god, surely, Veronica, you must know that,"—his words became curiously intense as he lifted his head—"light, the eternal enemy of darkness. An illiterate mercenary, smitten with Parthian arrows on the low plains of Scythia, will forget the polished silver of the belly of Roman Venus. Light, they can hardly ignore, severing as it does their hours of duty, their space of enforced marches, beating upon them in the flame of unholy destruction and warning them on the peaks of the Indian Himalayas. Rome is all-powerful in its greatness—"

Veronica interrupted his discourse: "Obviously Fabius."

Veronica could not have explained why the intensity of his words at just that instant, froze her. She herself had begun an argument, in such manner, earlier in the afternoon. The image of a Cretan tulip-god, however, had warmed her, set her by fire-lit altars. The purity of this abstract Mithra, as Nobilior spoke of him, chilled her. Was she piqued simply, fearful, lest her own revelation be dismissed by Fabius? She became unaccountably again the sophisticated intellectual.

"Love has gone from us, Fabius" she stated with apparent irrelevance. "I mean for us, there is no help in loving, or hating, or hurting. We are beyond the petty enjoyments of the circus, and the intellectual efforts of the Academy repel us. Where are we?"

Fabius believed he had said nothing of love. In some subtle manner, Veronica had stung through the "plate-metal" of his externalized abstraction. He realised, it was not purely of abstractions, he was speaking. This new cult of light, personified in Mithra, he confessed to himself, presented a personable image. Was it a love-god simply? Not love, displayed wantonly at any market-corner and in the halls of modish Romans; this Love was an apostate.

Fabius' experiments had been, for the most part, among witty and disillusioned members of his own class. He had thought in Veronica, the Etruscan, to have found a return to the old mode; she was fine and hardy, intense, subtle, like some thin Ionian Aphrodite—but Aphrodite?

"Yes, Veronica, you see something of the matter that has touched me." Veronica hardly knew what gesture or turn of speech of Fabius' had fired her; some aloof mood, alien to him, had undermined her discovery, her return to some personable Image—an Image that held flower-bud to famished lips, that was no Greek Eros but stood, heady and alive, in blossoming wild-grass.

"I mean, Fabius, any savage may worship light, as differentiated from darkness. Light is light, we know that. The meanest savage knows that. The Greek, though, who first made Light personable in the figure of some marble stripling, was profiting the human race far more than any abstract philosopher." She found herself compelled to put forward names of sculptors, dramatists, poets. "Surely a Leucadian Apollo, spread with ivory and gold, or later Delphic athlete, has manifested man to God and God himself to man." Her field of red wild-tulips seemed about to be blighted by Fabius' outside Image; she could not know what it was that suddenly had her arguing for Hellenized divinities. Earlier that afternoon, she had seemed to intimate they could be banished by a Cretan song-girl's magic.

"Mithra," she said again. She did not know what had overcome her. She did not specifically want Fabius, yet she did not want to lose him. "Mithra," she thought, "has nothing to do with women."

She said, "There seems to be something in the air. I can't describe it. Everyone talks of something. With Mnevis really, it's a sort of poet, a young Jew. I almost forgot to tell you."

"A young—?"

"Jew."

"—how can he be a poet?"

"You may well ask. Hebrew, the language of the old prophets is, of course, of no use to a progressive modern thinker. He speaks Aramaic but naturally has composed nothing in that dialect."

"Naturally—"

Veronica was standing. Her eyes, though she was facing the half-open curtains, were blotted out, he again noted, with that odd light, the depth of a black crystal. Her eyes again astonished him. Was it possible—

"Veronica, you don't, I presume, experiment?"

"Experiment?"

"Certain of our Roman ladies seek out Arabs, wandering Orientals—you don't ever—"

Her laughter always pleased him, it made her that creature of avid converse, whose rhythms recalled wind on water, or long space of sand; a silver lilt of notes and his heart was back in the cavern of last night's (was it only last night's?) experience.

Again, Fabius' eyes were heavy with the smoke of many candles. He recalled minute details of the emotional ritual; strangely, he did not differentiate these emotions from his feeling for the woman opposite. He saw now, that Veronica's stark beauty hinted at nothing of the opium-sleeper; she dreamt of high things, of light, as she herself had intimated, that reflected across polished marble, fell and was refracted back, in limpid waters. Hers, was no Oriental ecstasy.

Again, Fabius Nobilior found that he could hold her, in his thoughts, as he remembered the litany; the communion-cup of red wine, the remoteness of the chosen cavern, the simplicity of the night, the astonishing grandeur of those many stars he rarely noticed, save on occasion of forced march or of unusual peril. Spilt blood of the ritualized bull-sacrifice again intoxicated his sense, along with the uncanny certainty that, out of the dense recess of that mountain cavern, that very symbol of beauty and perfection was about to emerge.

Lovers of beauty, the "love-brothers" joined in peril and unwonted physical achievement, had knelt to receive the wafer of fine meal that was stamped with the cross, that early symbol of the Star and hence eternity. The symbol of the love of father and son, the Light and the Star, of Beauty and Purity, undefiled by battle scar and stain of physical degradation, had somehow miraculously touched him. Fabius Nobilior fell in love, as did the roughest soldier of his regiment, with an idea simply—the idea of a brother-lover pure and undefiled in beauty, the direct son of an eternal father. But that love, Fabius now found, did nothing to distract from this: Veronica staring, wide-eyed and passionless, into the waning sun-light.

He was obsessed now with his Light, with his Darkness. The appeal to some super-sense that the returned mercenaries had first yielded to—in high plateau and above rivers bordering Indus—had no remote bearing on the pre-Augustan cycle, the "old gods" that Caesar had summarily commanded to be re-instated. Latium and Tuscany had little to contribute to this region of the super-conscious or the sub-conscious that this one being, Mithra, so definitely had entered.

"Veronica, as the slain beast and the cries of his dying somehow purified the very hollow of that secret mountain-cavern, so—so—" (he, so adroit with Alexandrian parallel, stumbled toward expression) "—so, so Love. Isn't this mere act of our unity only a prelude to another?"

Her eyes alone answered. In their brilliance, Fabius seemed again to see candles set upright against black rock. He recalled the knife edge of the dawn, inserted as it were along the outline of the rim of distant mountains. He felt again pre-sentiment that *this* time when the sun rose, God actually would rise with it. In the same way, he now felt actually that Love had again flowered, and God was part of it—not materially, but (he sought for the right image) as the aura of fragrance is to a flower-head. He touched her. "*Sparge rosas,*" he whispered, still thinking of the white roses of immaculate dew that had lain heavy on those fields, as they knelt to hail the Sun— Mithra, pure light—as he climbed above the mountains.

"*Sparge rosas,*" he again insisted, half out of pity for her apparent state of cold intensity, "have you forgotten—love, Veronica?"

V

It seemed to her, that was the one thing she was the most unlikely to forget, and yet, not exactly. Did she want to forget? She could not imagine life severed from physical contact; on the other hand, those contacts meant nothing to her, without contrast. Mnevis was that contrast. She could come from Mnevis, raise Fabius to some unwonted pitch of jealousy—for he was obviously more jealous of this woman than he had ever been of either Memnonius or Pilate (who after all, hardly counted).

Of old, he had been peculiarly insensitive to any sort of intellectual provocation; she had, for fun, tried him. But now Fabius—who, after all, was arguing so fiercely, for a sort of ideal brother-love—seemed especially to resent one thing in her: the discovery of an ideal sister. That, he could not stand. He had pretended to be relieved when she had said, it was no man that had inflamed her. But he was not. He did not, it was quite clear, like her liking Mnevis.

He had showed it in a way men have, of being somewhat stubborn in insistence, seeming concerned only for her happiness, and then becoming wistful. That was one thing she hated. Fabius was a soldier. She could bear weakness, in Memnonius, who was only a half-man; after all, he was only an Egyptian. But Memnonius, though physically much the frailer, had a stubborn core of hardness. He didn't ask for the sort of sympathy men demanded, as if they were children, left out. Everything is completely different, she mused, with each one. Why can't we simplify things – lover, husband – to the rôle of the new comedy? But no. None of that quite worked. It was, she was certain, that the world needed a new sort of lover, exactly a new lover. Fabius, apparently, had found him and yet, what he said of this new cult of Mithra, left her out. "It leaves," she repeated to herself, for the hundredth time since Fabius' departure, "out, women."

Fabius had slid through the curtains, without lifting them, as was his manner, when he was a little anxious about her. Well, everyone knew he had been here and how long he had stayed. Why did they all go on pretending? Of course, it would be impossible, if they started not to pretend. Life would require too much explanation, the whole contour of the social world about her, would change. And, she said to herself, we are too tired, too lazy. We don't want to change. Fabius comes to me, or Memnonius comes. Pilate's chief concern is their political affinities. I don't care to know where Pilate goes, nor whom he sees, so long as he is courteous to me (and he is that, always), before strangers. He is courteous to me, even when we're alone, but that's because he's lazy, because I am lazy; it would cost us both too much effort to adjust to the crude banality of reality.

There was nothing real in this life, that's what it was. She had said "the banality of reality," but it would have been more accurate to call it "the banality of *unreality*." Anyhow … the banality of the particular brand of unreality, that her world offered.

Yet one thing, more or less, convinced her of reality. It was love. If that goes, what is there left? She shuddered. She had to face this thing. She didn't want Fabius and she didn't want to lose him. It had been the same, some time past, with Memnonius. They both had served a purpose. But she was no Pasiphae of legend, to desire a man as if he were a beast. She was no sorceress. She wanted both men. Nor am I, she thought, Circe. These men do not turn into swine, nor do they turn me into anything less than myself. But what is myself?

One person had troubled to define her and certainly had succeeded up to a point, and that was Mnevis. Fabius hadn't really. Memnonius had thrilled her curiosity. Fabius had let her alone, at least, as far as intellectual pursuits were concerned. He had thought, or thought that he thought, her friendship with Mnevis, in the end, had something to do with a drug or opiate. She hadn't, she realized, actually thought of drugs or opiates, until Fabius mentioned it; but now that she did, she remembered Memnonius had offered her some escape from terror once, when it was decisively reported that a new and loathsome disease was making headway in certain quarters of the city. Its physical effects were horrible. Memnonius had said, "There is a way out, Veronica."

She hadn't taken the small phial he offered. He said the action of the potion was instantaneous. She was afraid—out of indifference or curiosity or satiety—she might one day simply snap the fine end of the glass-phial and pour it in her wine-cup. She didn't want death, really. She wanted an answer. Her curiosity would keep her from danger of this sort.

But when Fabius hinted at his suspicion, she saw he had a reason. After talking with this Mnevis, fire ran through her veins and into her skull. The woman was perhaps, herself, an opiate. There was no comparison between what she felt for Mnevis, and what she felt for these men. It was different. She had said, "I am done with Fabius." But if she had, the more exquisitely, yielded to him, it was that she might, the more exquisitely, retain him. Veronica never let go a lover. Fabius would have his secret niche, or pedestal, somewhere, within her inner Temple. She was neither ashamed nor enriched by this discovery. "Fabius may yet serve me."

She whispered, "Asterios," wondering why the name had taken such deep root in her being. She returned to Mnevis, to her strange cult and her stranger credulity. Mnevis' credulity was oddly enriched by letters, numbers, her odd infatuation. Veronica, lying in her half-dream, recalled words that, earlier, had seemed written on smooth metal; so clear, so hard, so concise had been the phraseology of this Mnevis, that (lying there, her spirit calm, her psyche, quivering and alive, like sea-fish under water) Veronica could almost, with a separate eye or entity, draw her experience nearer.

Mnevis had spoken casually, yet in so suave and so sustained a manner, that the cult of this new Master of Israel, of the just-discovered—or rediscovered—Asterios, seemed equally applicable and stimulating. Asterios was, it was obvious, Adonis or even Hyacinth; the name *Asterios*—a Hellenized version of re-mote Cretan origin—brought with it new significance. Asterios, himself, seemed to be quivering round them.

"—there seems to be something in the air," she remembered saying earlier to Fabius. Fabius too—and Mithra. Mithra, taken all in all, it seemed to Veronica, must be another Asterios, another star, but a cold star. A cold star but the same star; for this later, bull-sacrifice suggested earlier, Cretan bull-rites or Dionysiac ritual. Veronica recalled exquisite phrase of that flower-festival: *consider the lilies of the field,* and wondered in just what connection she had heard it. Lilies of the field? Red tulips were not the only ones, but what lily was more radiant and more specifically of the field than those small glazed single blossoms? Veronica said *lilies of the field*, half sleeping, and recalled in a sort of dream that it wasn't chorus of Dionysiac ritual; it was that Jew of Mnevis.

The Jew of Mnevis seemed to be visibly before her.

She did not see the man, really in her eyes, she did not see him. She reconstructed, from the fire, the white intensity of the love of Mnevis for this Master, as she called him, something like him. No, it was not that Jew, she saw, nor any Oriental; though, as a matter of fact, the small image that came to her was, in its way, essentially occult, different from the Roman and even Greek effigies of lost and barely surviving deities. It was a tiny statue. Well, not so small, she thought; one could not measure an impression such as this. Her memory was of a small, archaic statue, in the disused temple in the garden of her Etruscan father. It was neither small nor large, really, it might be a tiny *objet d'art*, like any of the miscellaneous collection, in her dressing-room and boudoir. Or it might be gigantic, like a Capitoline Jupiter. Really, if you measured it, she supposed it was small. But then, she was herself small.

Her memory, Pilate often told her, was a curious prodigy. Her mind, he told her, did not work like a Roman's, and Memnonius said, she was worse than a Greek. Memnonius had said, "Etruscans are vipers—Jews almost"; perhaps that was the link. Etruscans were like Jews for their starkness and stubborn intensity. Yet they borrowed. That small god of her childhood, that no one in her memory had worshipped, was neither Greek, Roman, nor Egyptian, yet it hinted at all these. It was, for all its borrowed paraphernalia (its Greek

peplum folded in the archaic matter, its Egyptian primitive-
striding right foot), not Greek, nor Egyptian. It hinted even
of some crude, early native Roman ware, in the finish of the
metal—but that metal-work actually, the Romans had borrowed from Etruria. The statue took and gave back; it was a
mass of contradictions and yet, for all that, the little image
retained something apart, original, authentic.

Wasn't it like that, with the Jew of Mnevis?

Veronica remembered every word that Mnevis had
quoted: those sayings, authentic or otherwise, of that Master.
They were just there, those words, as separate and defined as
the collection of small bronzes on the low shelf beyond the
curtain, or the various adornments of her dressing-table.
They were metal, chaste, with flower-bud and lily and dove
and serpent, not unlike really, the work of her forefathers.
The Jew cut words from metal, but he worked with live material. Souls, really. Veronica remembered so many things
(her life—full of memory): concise images, but borrowed, ornate, she thought, like all that trash out there in the reception-room, or the bottles on this table. She lay on the divan,
her feet parallel, like a bride or a dead lady, done in stone under a tall cypress. Yes, I am a dead lady. I was alive a moment
since, seemingly wild with the kiss of Fabius. But that was
the last. I am dead now.

No. I am not dead. My mind goes on and on, like some
silly mechanical trumpet-note before a battle. My mind
sounds in me, like a trumpet. All the silly things are equally
authentic; if I could forget the silly little bright things I've
said. How I used to surprise Pilate for fun: "the elder Va-
lerius' second wife had peridot rings, not agate," or "the third
ambassador, on the occasion of the banquet of Lucius Gaius,
quoted Pompeius Trogus not the Pompey of Alexandria."

Impertinence all that, a way of being funny; but it amused Pilate.

But in this new remembering, there was something different. Every phrase of that Jew opened a door. Veronica was free enough, it was obvious, in her ordinary life; she could do what she wished. In return for her often surprisingly astute subtlety, and support in various diplomatic matters, Pilate had frankly given her the run of the town. He knew, she would for her own sake, as well as for his, make no vulgar *faux pas*. She was too consummate an artist for that.

All the same, doors that open outwardly, in this life, sometimes have a peculiar, almost automatic habit of slamming shut. But they do not, Veronica mused, open in and out; perhaps they are curtains, she said, or wide portals that roll backward. The doors of her mind moved sideways, Janus-shaped—as they led out, they shut in. What was the use—all her hectic experimenting? Well, there was one purpose. To show, she smiled gravely, there was no use.

O, there was some use in all that. It was all a show, a good-enough show, put over. But what had she got out of it? No answer to any question. What I wanted, she considered, with her eyes now staring at the blurred pattern of that bright ceiling—fitting background for her ape when he chose to leap and run along the rod of the dividing curtain—"what I want," she said, now aloud, "and always wanted, was an answer." She wondered, apropos of the half-deciphered design of leaf and painted leaf-shape, where now, was that Bes? I haven't seen him, for days. Sometimes when she was away, she left him with her Greek slave, always on guard, outside. That man, a sort of poet, had quoted Aristophanes, but then, all those slaves did quote Greek plays. Something from a play with which she was unfamiliar, bees and wasps ruling a universe.

Bes was that Bee.

I am that flower. What flower? Not the roses of Fabius' definition. *Sparge rosas,* he had said on leaving. She had begged him to go out quickly. She had known, as he kissed her and laid a small, heavy head on a pillow—like a head of marble cut off from its body, laid on a strip of dark cloth (her pillow)—that if he, if anyone, could get that head functioning with that body, there would be no *Vale. It was always Ave, Vale,* one or the other. This time, it was *Ave.*

Not so much, to the actual idea of the young Jew Mnevis spoke of. No doubt, at close range, he would be disappointing. Anyhow, what use had Jews for women? But that was the whole point. From the first, Mnevis had insisted that this was some sort of paragon who loved women, yet was no lover. What was a lover? What sense did that make? It belonged to some fabulous state of innocence…. Could one go back?

Unless ye become as—as what was it, Mnevis said, he said we were to become? Birds, lilies—something else—ah—a child.

If I became as a child, there is something I want. I know there is one thing. That is where this Jew of Mnevis, and Memnonius with his "Etruscans are Jews," came together, the two streams of thought—her Roman consciousness now, and the almost forgotten, yet ever present, Etruscan background. Two streams of thought became one stream; an Etruscan may be a Jew, and that Jew—no that Etruscan—was my father.

Not really, so much my father. There was the second wife and her heavy-handed servants, who had pushed out the little old gods and decorated a Campanian Venus or sort of blousy Juno, with scentless mallow. It was an offering Veronica, as a child, had felt, all out of key with their house. The small statues had fitted into their nooks. These lamps and gew-gaws did not. So she had lost her father.

But no, I never lost him.

He turned into a statue, she saw, as she recalled the reference to lilies. "Consider the lilies," she said. He had turned into the small secret image, that, as a child, with brothers, one smaller and one larger—she had paid respect to. It was a game, at the same time, it was worship. One could not tell really, anymore, where one begins, the other leaves off. But she was sure, that there was more reality in their simple games of high-priest and high-priestess and the chaplets woven from what flowers they could beg from their good friend the gardener, than in that Campanian's fat ox. It had been a very big ox, not one, fortunately, from their farm. These were too small, almost wild, the woman had despised them. She had despised everything.

Poor woman. Veronica thought, "Poor woman," for now in retrospect, with two separate streams of consciousness blurred into a pleasant affable state of half-dream, of half-reality, she felt she knew precisely, that her life, in the end, must have held bitterness. For she never had my father, why no, she never had our father. How was it? Were there children? And if so, what sort of children? There never was another girl anyhow, to rival—to rival—

But no, there was no rivalry. The new wife had our father. We had the little statue.

It came to life now. Was she sleeping, awake? Half of her mind woke, and she thought, "This is phantasy, impossible, I love my father." Half of her mind slept, and she thought, "Fabius is rid of, at last. I really didn't want him." Somewhere else, someone remembered, a gypsy-woman who had followed her, a girl on a visit to relatives in the city, predicting a glorious future. They always predicted that, and yet that is what she had. Why, said Veronica to herself, half-sleeping, as if she just now realised it, "I am the wife of Pilate."

There was a dream somewhere.

Somewhere a dream was waiting. It had to do with the statue of course, and the statue was a Jew—no, it was the man who was a Jew, that Jew of Mnevis; the statue was (she had figured it out upon sleeping), a mixture of unrelated race expressions, yet made one in a final solution, called Etruscan. So she. Why, every Etruscan is a half-breed, worse than these Greek slaves. We know more than any Roman, but unlike these Greeks, we have the astuteness of the serpent (Memnonius said), we hide it. We have cold, calculating exteriors, he said, and we make money, or did; we turned everything to metal, like the old king in the fable … Midas … Each is a sort of Midas. Someone touched my father and his smile froze, on an instant. It was a hard little smile; he was no doubt thinking of his new wife's fat, Campanian dowry.

He wasn't thinking of that. He was thinking of our mother. So the smile that might have been lascivious, was tender; the tenderness, that might have been merely banal, was exquisite. He would always be caught in the act of smiling. Then, as if to excuse the grimace, the eyes were tilted at the corners to make the mask as ridiculous as those bird-faces that that Greek slave had informed her, were worn in another of those comedies: *The Birds? The Bees?* There was all that in his face. His statue's smile conveyed everything and he was a sort of centre to their garden; banished, he had given

intensity to the corner of the field where she and her brothers played at being high-priests. They had demanded an answer from the small upright image. But it did not give it.

I was always waiting for an answer.

The girl, Mnevis, gave it.

The Jew of Mnevis gave it.

But of course, that is impossible; they are transients, va-
grants; you can't freeze his smile, like the smile of my Etruscan; you can't set her in a niche, fixed mother-image ...
They will be lost ... I'll see them again ... see her again ... why
−I haven't seen him. He is so clear. As clear as my little image.
If my image should speak to me, give me an answer, it would
be in the words of that Jew ... Memnonius gave me the idea
that Jews were vipers, like Etruscans ... *Be ye wise as*−

But things became fluid in her half-dream, were lost.
There seemed nothing for it. If things flowed on and past,
things vivid, vital, like running water, they were lost. Catch
them, they freeze and give no answer. Yet in a half-dream, it
seemed almost possible that the flowing rhythm of thought
could be fixed for ever, made static, permanent, like terse
Delphic utterances. *Consider the*−birds? lilies?

Fabius had said she didn't value her jewels. One gesture, he
had said; if Pilate lifts a finger, they're lost. But Pilate would-
n't lift a finger. They would never be lost. Her jewels were
thoughts frozen ... frozen adoration. Yes, Pilate really loved
her. She had never gotten near him. But had she gotten near
those others? ... The jewels were now fluid, iridescent, were
cold dew that dripped across her bare feet, as she ran early in
the morning, before sunrise to her statue.

Gold, she remembered (like realities racing now in her
head), and silver had been variously in-set, for his crown. She
could steady herself in her dream, could almost set merchant's

value on the plunder that someone later thought worthy to pick out. She had woven a blossoming branch to replace the metal. They had peeled off the silver; now he was like a Pan set on a tree, in an orchard. She believed she loved the statue better, after it lost its value.

Its value? … Values. What was the value of the little cast-off image? Wild-pear buds might have matched jewels, prised out of the crown-rim … Not pearls … Pearls were too subtly pure and untarnished, for an Etruscan's headdress. It was gold filigree-work and silver. They could make anything of metal.

It was speaking to her. It was about to speak now, to her. She always knew it would speak. She had asked it so many questions. But it was Mnevis who was speaking.

She was back in the room (was it yesterday?) with Mnevis.

"He has at the moment no visible place of dwelling. He names himself, among the wild beasts; a fox, he says, has as much right to habitation, as a man. A fox has its hole, he says, or a vulture its cranny. He speaks of the flight of birds, as giving visible prophecy and mystery. He says, study the birds and you shall gain oracular divination. Not bird oracle, as long practised by Greek and Asiatic. The Prophet does not mean investigation of the intestines of dead or half-dead birds. He says, study the bird in flight and by its pass and sway across a dark or across a sun-painted heaven, you may read hieroglyphs and signs and oracles. As this parchment spread on this common table" (Mnevis' numerical reading was then, just finished) "so the sky is. The sky, he says, is a parchment and the message of any bird, flying across it, has more meaning than any craft of priesthood. By this argument, this Jesus affirms his cult of mere humanity. Each man, he claims, is a priest and, since no bird can fall without the knowledge of the supreme Diviner, so no man, with like cognizance, can falter.

"He believes that flowers too, opening, speak further of mystery in the curling back of their petals. The Prophet has enjoined his followers to study flowers, those wild lilies in particular, that—red and blue, crimson and kingly purple— open wide to the sun-rays along the Galilean foot-hills. By minute contemplation of the unfolding of a wild-flower, you gain, he claims, hieratic knowledge of the inner mystery. Instead of confining this knowledge to the temple and the somewhat forbidding line of the initiate, the Jew says *all* are initiates. The heaven is open to all who read. But realizing that Babylonian and adept Assyrian doctrine has already spread knowledge concerning the power of planet and star and sun and moon, this one confines his mystery to cycles less well known. Simpler, yet in their very simplicity, more deeply mysterious. Like the Eleusinians, he calls to mind the grain, its sowing, its reaping, the manifold beauty of its various stages of growth and of its final medium—death, or new life, which completes re-birth on the earth-plane, with foreknowledge of the heavenly.

"Not in opposition, but rather in affirmation of the cult of star and meaning of the eternal circle of the heaven, he claims that no bird shall fall, no grass-blade pierce the earth, no grain rise and uncurl stem and leaf and fruit, no serpent lift a head and no dove spread fan-tail or unfold wing-feather, without the conscious and intimate knowledge of the supreme Diviner, who is the father of wind and bird and man equally. He is an entity so all-inclusive, that literally *no bird can fall* without the most intimate inter-relation of psychic vibration."

Psychic-vibration? Veronica now recalled how Mnevis had paused there as if baffled at last by her expression of divinity.

That particular phrase, "psychic-vibration," had remained curiously fixed in the mind of Veronica, the gem as it were to the whole circle, the whole philosophy that Mnevis had so subtly, with such exquisite choice of phrase, outlined for her. "Psychic-vibration" had recalled "the eyes of the psychic-gifted"—that phrase of Memnonius that, so well-turned and yet so awkwardly expressed, had seemed to fix her attention as one flawed pearl will in a necklace of monotonously matched, perfect specimens.

"You have the eyes of the psychic-gifted, like" (Memnonius had qualified) "Mnevis."

There *was* sympathy between them. Memnonius was never wrong in matters of matching. Veronica, still in the daze of her half-sleep, recalled how she had been wont in the early days of their intimacy to consult him on lesser matters: cosmetics, jewels, the ardour and power of gems and gem-clusters in hammered metal. These things had been so much tinsel and vanity between them yet, between them, they had worked toward higher subtlety. Veronica recalled her own antics, as one recalls, half-indifferently, those of a witty stranger; her pseudo-sophistication over matters of cosmetics, kohl, powdered galena or the fabulous chrysocolla.

Memnonius, the Egyptian legate, was then summoned often to her boudoir, not because of any formal amicable relationship—as that, for example, witnessed lately between Fabius and her husband—but for these more personal matters. Ladies of no recognized world were encouraged to dramatize imaginative ardour. Her imagination seethed within her, corroded; yet she projected something of her real self in this court-comedy with Pilate. With Memnonius to help her, for a time, she had gone on literally "dressing" for various ceremonials, like an actress, taking cue from him, acting across crowded rooms and into the very speeches of dull legates. Memnonius had shown her that her hidden histrionic talent could be utilized and enjoyed, even though she had but one auditor—himself, so acting with her.

Memnonius, at the same time, sustained her interest in religious festival by showing how the old form had been revitalized, made accessible to the world at large by the Greek, who intellectualized pure religious precept. He had been wont to remind her too, that certain Greek festivals of the late archaic period required ladies, even of high birth, to sustain some character, to "act" literally. That that character was a goddess— Ceres or her daughter—or a heroine of mythology, didn't alter the fact that it gave opportunity for fantastic head-dress, painted fingers and fabulously exaggerated jewels.

Later again there were royal customs, he had reminded her, that permitted ladies to form circles and dance, even if somewhat restricted and in somewhat stately measure. Here, it was stated, even in Jerusalem, in the strict seclusion of the home, the palace of her father, the daughter of the queen Herodia, displayed no small talent. Veronica's dramatic gift, that they had at first discussed so openly, soon gave way to another, more subtle. She was, in his phrase, one of the psychic-gifted. Memnonius' words—along with certain of the fine sentences, quoted by Mnevis—remained, as it were, oddly incised with delicate precision in her brain.

Mnevis was wonderful. She had appealed to some latent imaginative fervour in Veronica, just as that Mithraic bull-rite in the mountains, had struck open some door, till now closed fast, in Fabius. Intellect, and Augustan precept, had been welding doors. The cult of the returned old gods had set the polite world to thinking, and fresh thoughts had wrought fresh barriers. There was no "metal clangour" of intellect, however, in these last experiences. Veronica somehow knew that she and Fabius had now, for all their outward dissimilarity, struck some new life in common. She returned to the thought of Fabius.

Yet Veronica realized, at the same time, Mnevis held something rarer than Fabius (even at his best, in the early glamour of their infatuation, with his fine, literary precept). *Purpureo narcisso* had fallen curtly, on occasion of proffering that same intoxicating bloom, her winter favourite; his *calathis ariusia nectar* would fill in a halting sentence, seeming to dash white fire of healing in her wan face, at a moment when throne-room ceremonial had seemed about to suffocate her. Fabius flung roses deftly, it is certain, but it seemed, in light of this tulip-gatherer, this Jew, with his undifferentiated "lilies," that here was something rarer, even with his artistic formulas, for all that honeybees hovered, almost it seemed visibly, on the suave lips of Fabius, quoting Tibullus or his favourite Propertius.

Fabius' words were deeply resonant, his tone soothing, his utterance held quality of winged things. *Ariusia nectar.* Veronica had been, for a time, meshed in a net of blossom; flower tangled her, name of remembered fruit-tree, his *roscida mala* and *Meliboe pirus* to whose branch, in flower, he exquisitely contrasted her. She was lost in a lesser magic.

Rousing herself from voluptuousness that, with Fabius' exquisite tact, had never seemed too much, a net visibly held her—black butterfly, marked with vermilion and painted, at the wing-tip, with Egyptian azurite. Her painted wings would flutter, then die slowly. That anguish had tended to sustain her, bright drug composed equally of stinging fire and opiate. Veronica had so sustained her spirit. She had kept up her intellectual aspiration, and her vanity, with ceremonials of no slight importance with her husband. That third element, compound of all things subtle—her suppressed will toward self-expression, the artist latent in her that had, at one time, been supported by Memnonius—had lately again, been re-vitalized by Mnevis.

"Her hair," Veronica irrelevantly noted, as she now deliberately roused herself, awake to time and its contingencies, "is cap of shadow. In shadow, it is jet. In the light, it becomes bronze, almost."

The eyes she knew too, were deceptive (Veronica ordered her maid to set-to with the hair-dressing), neither grey nor blue. Well, she would go back to Mnevis.

VI

Mnevis said, "888, the Jew, the secret Prophet has that most accurate number, the absolute and final number in all chronology. There is no further materialization possible." Veronica listened. She found the woman to-day, somewhat colourless. Her room lacked something —its spirit; what just, Veronica wondered, was it?

Firstly, it was easily recognizable that the light marred mystery within doors. There were none of the usual candles that, even by day, Mnevis had been wont to light, drawing the curtain, preliminary to secret, inner conference. There was no faint tang of incense. But the intangible thing that Veronica hadn't yet formalized, now came to her, as we sometimes miss a familiar servant only when his place is taken by another. Subtlety is often barely noticed, till it's quite gone. There was something *not* in the room—a spirit or being of repose—there was no repose, everything seemed dry, spiritually dusty. Now that it was gone (familiar body-servant), Veronica recognized it.

She endeavoured to focus, to seize on the various layers of the inner magic, the things that made it definite, definable. She realized in a moment, in no vague terms, the various phases of her infatuation.

She had been infatuated first, with the dusk in this small chamber, the half-light, punctuated with flare of candles, the lily that had flowered singly in the flat bowl, the cross—the cross, she noted suddenly, was not there.

"The cross that used to hang there?"

Mnevis answered, "It was marked with symbols of ancient ritual."

Veronica repeated, "Ancient ritual? But isn't that what profits us here? Isn't it ritual that has helped you all along, in your discernment?"

Mnevis repeated, "Yes, ancient ritual. But," she faltered, "the cross was just an arabesque with curious sigil: names and inter-laced letters, serpent and rose."

Veronica said, she didn't see how that mattered. Mnevis answered that she wanted something different. "The cross itself dates far back. I want something new. I have found it."

When Veronica asked her what it was she had found, Mnevis answered, "The oldest possible—yet the strangest, most unaccountable thing. A new way of loving." That, Veronica answered, would interest her deeply.

Mnevis returned to the contemplation of numbers that she had inscribed on fresh papyrus. The paper was crisp, unbroken, with no dark thread to mar the fibre of the surface. Mnevis had a mania about perfecting her star-writing; her script, with Veronica's numbers and star-numbers, was marked here and there with additions, and here and there, most carefully corrected.

Mnevis had written her 888 with no intermediary of incense, candle or ancient cross. She was clear in her purpose. Everything today, it seemed to Veronica, had become trite, material; Mnevis was using her star-knowledge and computation for another purpose.

"Well ... tell me ..."

"I've been trying to tell you. But you would interrupt about the cross and lilies. I tell you, I don't want intermediaries."

"Does it matter," asked Veronica, "what we use, so long as

we get there?" Mnevis was firm on this point. She had experimented, Mnevus explained. She re-explained to Veronica. "I thought we could get back the old divinities. I see now it's impossible."

Veronica said, "The old divinities have never left us, never will leave." Mnevis answered they *would* go, if one could dispense with antique symbol. If once the dove, the lily, the cross, the goblet and the ritual of communion (as now practised) could be done away with, one would return straight to divinity. There was no need of intermediary.

"Perhaps so, you might just as well say you can only seek your lover in one garment—sackcloth. What does it matter, whether one partakes of the sacrament of ecstasy clothed or un-clothed? Do a few pearls about a bare throat matter?" "No—" Mnevis was, it appeared now, troubled. "But you don't understand."

Veronica said, "Since when have we so signally demurred at the passion of Aphrodite?"

Mnevis said, "I don't demur at anything. But we want something different. A new religion must have no crown and mitre. It must have no line of doves ascending or descending, it must have above all no cross—that insidious image dating before man, that has now returned from Thoth. It came by way of the Greek Hermes, and came again to the Mithraic cave-cult, obliterating possibility of new power, new sets of symbols. We must have above all, no cross. That's why I have removed it."

Veronica still waited for the final revelation. "Well, it wouldn't hurt us to get rid of the glare. Why don't you draw the curtains?"

Mnevis moved toward the window. She was not, Veronica noted, as beautiful as she had imagined her, as she lay yesterday, on that pyre of ecstasy. Lying yesterday, worn out, yet illuminated, Veronica had seen this room as a sort of temple. She had come here unknown, and to her surprise, had gleaned strange rapture. She had recognized a high sort of loving, dangerous maybe, but the sort of clear-white passion that deified the earlier nymphs of Arcadian Artemis. Sister to sister, lover to lover, Veronica had loved Mnevis, as one grown tired of too much admiration, turns to view a familiar face, washed clear as in spring water, and realizes with no vanity that that face is one's own.

"Surely, there's a myth of some woman who loved—who loved—and bathed and found herself renewed and beautiful?" Mnevis appeared unapproachable, she didn't seem to listen. Veronica continued, "Yes, it was Hera—you remember?"

Mnevis didn't want to recall old ritual. She repeated that she wasn't in the mood for such things. Veronica stated, undaunted, "When I first came here, I was like that Hera. I don't know what you did to change me." Mnevis turned. Her face was unfamiliar, un-illuminated. "But—what *is* the matter?" Mnevis said, "He helped others—but himself, he could not." It was obvious she was quoting a line from some old parchment. Veronica could merely guess. "Well?" "His number is the number of the last illumination, the 8 and the 8 and the 8. Add them together you get 24, the 2 and the 4 added again, make 6, the number of all-loving."

"Ah," said Veronica enraptured, "then, you don't do away with your doves and lilies. He *is* another love-god." But as to that, Mnevis was quite certain. The Jew was in no accepted sense, a love-god.

Mnevis had said that she wanted something different. But
Veronica, attuned to the moment, realized in just that rare
flash of perception, that the past could in no way be im-
proved on. "You can't improve on the beauty of the already-
expressed—the Greek, our native Etruscan." Again she was
reminded of pear-buds, just not in blossom, those hard little
knots in the old silver-work; the filigree that had so perfectly
caught and frozen various lines, filaments of flower-stems.
Small frozen buds of orange and quince (if you cared to differentiate) and the live intertwining gold verbena. Gold and
silver were worked curiously, the filigree was frozen; the very
web of the spider could not be more delicate.

"The modern pompous new-art of the Capital has nothing to offer more exquisite than our old heirlooms. I never
found, among the modern works in Rome and Campania,
anything distantly to suggest the old Etruscan power and
delicacy. Yet the Etruscans too progressed from an old stem.
They wrought the casually recognizable Egyptian formula
upon silver plaque and platter and added something to it. So
here with these religions, philosophies, poetry."

Mnevis said, Veronica had completely missed the root of
the whole matter. The Jew, being an Oriental, yet of a certain
prescribed convention, had to seek patterns in another
medium. It was not art, concerned him. Where an Etruscan
workman might filigree gold on silver and copy Indian myr-
tle in turquoise, the pomegranate in redblood-stone, this
man worked with men's hearts alone.

"Alone? You speak as if men's hearts were the last and most

indifferent medium."

Mnevis didn't seem in a mood for talking. "Don't you see, if your Jew is a sort of metal-worker of humanity, melting, smouldering, re-casting Spirits, that he has the most magnificent medium to work with here—in Jerusalem? Here he has the most potent factors to content him." "To *content* him?" "Men from so many places, so varied in feature and spirit, of such depth of ignorance, such height of philosophic malleability, can nowhere else be found," Veronica surprisingly found herself asserting. "Just now in no other city. Jerusalem," she repeated, "is a perfect mystery for a mystery-monger," and she wondered at that last phrase. "Ah, Memnonius," she suddenly remembered, "he said, that first time he spoke of my coming to you, that you had friends among men of various *métiers* and with enchanters, his exact phrase was. Does Memnonius know the Jew then?" That, Mnevis couldn't or wouldn't answer.

Mnevis said, "The man comes and goes. I told you he had no habitation." But where, last time, Mnevis had chanted a paean to this Paragon, with lilt and fine flow of prophetic feeling, to-day her words fell silent; not with the upward wing of inspiration that seemed to flutter with visible light, when she last spoke of this same Prophet. Veronica repeated, "Then he *is* a sort of love-god."

That, Mnevis again resented. She moved here, there, listless, without apparent purpose, slipping her pen and her ink back into the little cupboard. Now she stood by the table where the flat bowl sat empty, not lighting (as was her way) the candles. Veronica feared intruding upon some secret, some psychic or emotional mood, from which Mnevis wanted to exclude her.

"You *do* want to exclude me?" "Exclude—?" "You are tired.

You can't always be up to your professional level of discrimination. Can't you be simple with me? I came as a friend to see you." "I don't know that I want friends among the associates of Caesar." "Caesar? Associates?" And Veronica remembered that she was a casual sort of sempstress, a hanger-on (in the rôle Memnonius had prescribed for her) from the outer circle of the outer circle of the court. "Surely—you can't think I am near enough to matter?" "That's just it—if you *were*—" "If I were?" "Well—we might ask you, then, to help us."

"Us," it appeared, was some two or three. There never were too many. The Master had prescribed a circle, a *two or three gathered together*. Such as followed the pilgrimages, into the mountains and by the lake and sea-side, were of a different persuasion. This Jew had his inner and his outer circles, like any other doctrinaire or teacher.

He had, like any peripatetic philosopher, his own set of rules, saying this to this one, while the others knew the words meant something different. "Seed," "harvest-time," "grain in the earth," the flower-bud and its way of opening: Mnevis had already explained to Veronica, each had its peculiar meaning. Well—it appeared now, that the people, enflamed some days since, had gotten them into trouble. Was it possible that Veronica, on her edge of court-intrigue and politics, had heard nothing at all about it?

Veronica repeated with sincerity, that she didn't believe the demonstration had been anything out of order—surely her—friend (a sort of personal attendant to one of the centurions) would have had something to say, if there had been anything out of the way. "*Had* he nothing to say about it?" Veronica assured Mnevis, "No, nothing–nothing, I tell you, has been said to me about it. What anyway *could* happen?" Mnevis repeated, "You don't know the priest-craft. He has openly annoyed them. He has offended their authority."

"But Mnevis," said Veronica, "the old rule of the Jew is ended. It was to settle matters of just such moment in an impartial assembly and without rigid religious prejudice, that my–that the Governor Pontius Pilate stays here." Mnevis had no faith in any governor. Some monster far off, seated in presumption of worldly authority, wringing extortionate tax from a crippled and underfed humanity. Her head was sunk forward, "an underfed humanity."

"Isn't humanity always that," asked Veronica, "how can you hope to give them anything?" She was surprised, had been amazed a moment since, to find the normally calm Cretan turned hysterical. Why had she, anyway? Veronica had looked up to this younger woman as a sort of priestess. Like any priestess, Veronica must admit, Mnevis was nothing, without her row of candles. This was obviously, one of her days off.

"I told you you needn't make yourself prophesy and discriminate for me. But is that any reason why we shouldn't be quite–simple?" Veronica found this Mnevis, an anomaly. She was a puzzle to her. Unused to the lapses of the common world about her, Veronica was puzzled. Herself in such predicament, she would draw close her curtains, give strict orders as to possible interruption, have the thing out in secret. Her husband Pilate, likewise, on occasion of more than usual mental perturbation, would perhaps summon one of his imperial chargers, have it out in another manner, alone, with just the barest possible attachment of body-servants, himself disguised frequently as one of his lesser officers.

At such moments, people of her world (Fabius, Memnonius) would, each and sundry, have his own ways: the high boot, the painted mask, each property adjusted in its own psychic way. Each had his own mask—wasn't that just it? Was that why Nobilior had shuddered: "mixing yourself up with that sort"? The mark of distinction—a certain manner available on each and every occasion—was patently unavailable to this Mnevis. The woman had no defence, no mask whatever. This struck Veronica suddenly as pitiable, and (being pitiable) in the worst of possible taste. To pity an object, in itself puts one in a false and awkward predicament. Veronica swiftly recovered herself for this unusual occasion. "I really want to help you."

The words, "I really want to help you," hadn't, in themselves, meant much. Veronica perceived intuitively, that they might now come to mean anything. She lifted her hand as if to wave away the matter. Her ring, unheeded for the first time, slipped from beneath the soft scarf folded on her lap and fell to the floor. She heard it clang almost like a pair of cymbals. Her sandal was too late to stop it. It rolled over the floor. Perhaps the too un-worldly Mnevis would not recognise that effigy, flat as a tortoise, an old seal, one of Pilate's favourites.

She might yet retrieve it, "That awkward phoenix," she said, "my friend's—"

"The—the *eagle*," gasped Mnevis. "Your—friend is something, then, peculiar?"

"Peculiar?" Veronica with a stiff effort to again recover, realised that she was the petty sempstress. She must not forsake her own part. She became trivial, light, found her laugh, some odd parody of affectation. "O—rather. Yes, he was rather—" she repeated again, marvelling at the vulgarity of her accent, at her ready-made answer, her appalling will toward this thing.

If Mnevis couldn't play her part, well, Veronica could act for them both. She had been wont frequently to help out a stumbling young dignitary this way. Where Mnevis lacked subtlety, poise, she would give it doubly, as her almost un-conscious habit was at any crowded assembly. After all, she saw now, there is only so much of everything, everywhere, in the whole of Rome and in Rome's provinces. Hence you might equally say, in the whole world, just anywhere. Where religion was strong, then politics were faulty; where politics mapped out, favourably civilising this same world with chart and road and dwelling (running water, open space in wide court-yards) then something else was so often, lamentably lacking. The spiritual, she noted, in a swift flash of intuition, must draw upon the material, as irrigation water from a river. Too much sheer spirituality makes for mal-adjustment. That was what Fabius formerly had warned her, "mixing yourself up with that sort." Mnevis was simply like a deformity, now, of mal-adjustment.

Veronica realising that the ring had done it, considered the flattened eagle, turning it this way, that way, then handed it back to Mnevis. "With this—something might be possible."

Mnevis took the ring, murmured, "No bird shall fall."

"No bird shall fall—" repeated Veronica, "not even the im-perial eagle. When you speak of a bird falling, when he, your Master, speaks of a bird falling, does he always mean the sparrow?"

Mnevis was a pitiable creature. She was shivering in this dull room—void within a void and nothing to mark time, to show anything of that afternoon, but this ring. It was clasped hysterically by Mnevis, who made a very picture of a Capitoline beggar. Vipers, beggars; Caesar had more than once commanded the imperial garrison to whip them off the stone steps leading to the forum. Mnevis was, it was evident, a sort of beggar.

Take away her stars, her chart, her psychic infallibility—and just what was she? Veronica had no manner of kindness, knew not what the word meant, her words were imperial and fitting the occasion. She repeated, "If no sparrow falls—what of the Roman eagle?"

This, Mnevis said, was mockery of no low order. It was malign and terrible. Didn't she understand the man they—they all adored, was in danger?

Veronica said, "What can we do to help him?" The imperial "we," slipping out unselfconsciously, put a new face upon the matter. Already Veronica realized she was committed, was being used by some force: Rome and the Eagle, this side; Beggar, Sparrow, that. Well, she was siding, all unconsciously, with the beggar though "we" for Veronica still meant: the *august* and imperial consort, *domina, augusta,* all that.

Veronica remembered her rôle, she hoped she achieved the right shade of not-too vulgar, in her parting words, "I'll ask my—*friend* to help you."

VII

Pilate's wife had promised, it appeared, to help. She had given her promise lightly, as they parted. The Jew was in all sorts of trouble, though Mnevis had insisted (this was the final horror) he needn't be, if he would accept the help they offered. What was that?

It appeared then, that there *was* some sort of force at work; Pilate had been right, speaking that day to Fabius in her boudoir. Veronica recalled their talk of Mithra and the Sun and the underground altars, where the soldiers gathered. Was it possible that the young Priest was one of them? It was more than possible that he was one of the Mithraic brotherhood, in spite of the Jewish dictums. But that, Mnevis had straightly contradicted. Mithra, she had insisted, was another foreign importation, a god from the Indus—the Jew had no dealings with any sort of outside deity. He believed (must she then repeat it?) in nature, the heart of man, the heart of God, both spirit, both unassailable.

Veronica had argued for a moment, before leaving. "That too, is the case of Mithra. That god's disciples, too, believe in a formula of initiation, and in spirit beyond body. Except for certain symbols (the priest and the body of the young god), they keep themselves apart from any sort of imagery; no carved images, just Light and then just Darkness." All that, Mnevis said again, was part of some Eastern cult, something of Indian origin. The Jew had fascinated her, it was evident. But Veronica continued, "He *is* a sort of sun-god."

Veronica, when she got back, flung herself down a few minutes before dressing. There had been the usual crowd at the
gate, attendants waiting to escort her. The parody of her incognito was well recognised, had been put to the test, long
since; the machinery of it was perfectly in order.

Veronica had passed the first guard and at the head of the
landing, drew back her veils. Pilate passed her at the second
landing; there was nothing of importance, he explained, a little matter, but it might delay him. Would she, in case of the
arrival of the second cortège of the Assyrian embassy, see to
the inner servants having the preliminary dancers ready, in
case he should be again delayed? There was pressing business
later. Veronica passed on, flung down the cloak, called for her
personal waiting-woman, repeated, "Don't let anything dis-
turb me."

Nothing, it was obvious, would do, for she was so tired. The
heat of the afternon had parched something deep within her.
She had gone blithely to this Mnevis, after her inward deter-
mination to break, at least physically, with Fabius. She had
recalled the sort of illicit glow of fervour on former occasion,
that trampling of the sheer exaltation of the intellect—that
clearing of the mind, *katharsis* of Aristotle, that was somehow, in some odd way, associated, as well, with the whole of
her early affectation of Platonic doctrine.

She had found repeatedly, that her endeavour toward Platonic perfection always flung her back, more intensely than

ever, into her old predicament. Veronica had firmly determined that the intellect was a curse, there was no facing love
with it. Yet certainly, she had discovered to her intense cha-
grin, love, for her at least, was still less satisfactory, without it.
Taken all in all, Fabius had been perhaps the most wholly
satisfactory. Inflamed with her predilection, however, toward
Fabius, she had sought this Mnevis, in love with an idea or
ideal–like marble gone cool, after sacrificial fire, ready for
different offering; flower-heads, the bowl of water.

Contrary to expectation, Veronica had found the seeress in
a dull mood. Mnevis had been in a dull mood. It might be
that sudden presumptuous flood of spring sunlight, presaged
a later torrid, blighting summer; or that the odd hour was
perhaps not one for this "psychic" business.

Veronica had noted, on the way to Mnevis, that the buds,
flowers were already parching. It was something really "in the
air" she thought, one of those early spring days that spread
bright scarlet and sudden purple prematurely, from jars and
garden-basins. Spring should be now–a virgin. She had
come to-day flaunting about the full-blooded rose and purple
of an early ornate summer. Mnevis' mood was perhaps due to
the sudden heat, a mere physical enervation. Mnevis was
simply tired out.

The wind would be rising later. It always did, after these
torrid heat-waves. She almost longed for that inevitable
thunder, which she usually hated. Fruit-branch half in bud
was already parched. She herself, spiritually likewise, was half
in bud, half parched, had longed for some final revelation.
But Mnevis instead of helping, was herself, for the moment
anyhow, also strangely wilted.

Though particularly "enervated," she did not trouble to
discard more than her outdoor garmets, burrowed deeper in

the pillows at the sound of feet and unaccustomed clang of metal from (she supposed) her inner courtyard. This business Pilate spoke of … her eyes closed heavily.

Desire begets its own alleviation. With the very spasm of thirst the mouth contracts, the throat shudders with nervous irritation. Desire begets; love begets. Whatever you want, you find, as surely as earth, dried out, must draw the ripe rain to it. Veronica was tired, she wanted—something. She knew as well as she had ever known to grasp at intuitive truth (as was her way, that Vera-ikon, Pilate even now called her)—that she had found the thing "almost" with this half-Cretan Mnevis.

Veronica was certain it was like looking in a mirror. Plato with his love and love, each a half, each about to find the other, seeking, searching, longing, was making the same statement. To Plato, it was possible to think of love finding its own complement. But Veronica saw it differently. No—to her each being was an entire entity, no half and half about it.

There would come a moment … there might come a moment in the life of each one of us, when the normal pulse is stilled by passion if it needs be; or healed and strengthened by mere normal tenderness; a moment when man says "woman is not enough," and woman says "man is not sufficient." That moment is a phase past mere Platonic intellectual enlightenment. There is—or is not—love contained within this germ of recognition, just as there may or may not be honey in the flower-head. The bee alone can discriminate. What can it matter to any one of us, whether this flower is fit for seed, this for fruit, or this for its mere blossom? The sheer beauty of a thing is, isn't it, its own excuse for being? "Consider," she said, as if from something half-remembered, "the lilies," and so fell numb and exhausted, sleeping.

On the edge of waking, she heard a voice. It said, "Veronica."

It was a voice she had heard in her early childhood, perhaps the voice of her father, or her elder brother, a voice barely discernible, perhaps it was even the favourite old gardener who called her (they had sworn to it and upheld it, even in later years) Veronica. Between sleep and waking, she heard her name, thought vaguely it was Pilate, saw as near her as the very curtain, the face of the sun Image. It was no longer smiling. The sheer intellectual beauty of the thing was obvious, apparent. It wore its wild-verbena. It bore a cloak (as was its usual manner) hung loosely on one shoulder, the other shoulder was bare. The voice would speak, it would always say "Veronica" ... verbena, Veronica, the two together. Verbena was the sacred herb, the herb of healing, with its intoxicating fragrance when the leaves were crushed between thumb and finger. The name was spoken, "Veronica." "I am Veronica," said Veronica, sitting upright.

She saw the room was empty; across the room, was the now half-drawn width of curtain. Someone had come to call on her, for a low lamp was lit for the heating of the irons, preliminary to her hair-dressing.

The oil was a sweet foreign importation, a scent she hadn't yet identified; it must have been that that had suggested the verbena—or vervain?—herbs crushed, the rush of feet on grasses. Veronica sat upright. Where were the palace servants? There was, it was obvious, confusion in the court beneath her. Had something really happened? Some gathering to view the foreign legation? Or simply that "little matter" that her husband had but lately assured her, was unimportant? She moved toward the curtained window.

Outside, a cluster of soldiers, a slight argument. Fortunately, Fabius Nobilior stood among them. A prisoner with face half-turned toward her, wore a wreath of blossom. The heavy branch was twined to make a crown. Veronica saw it was not blossom, it was the branch of the flowering-thorn— not yet in blossom or newly stripped of it.

The wife of Pilate leaned further from the window. There was some joke among them. The man standing was, it was obvious, replica of her dream. The dream had stood so clothed, peplum flung in the Greek manner, leaving bare a shoulder. The guard spoke somewhat lustily. Another voice, authoritatively commanded. Didn't they realize, broke in Nobilior, as if in final argument, that they stood under the window of the wife of Pilate?

That lady was making her way down, toward them. She had caught up a scarf, was still in her indefinite incognito garments, the ones discarded on entry, for these "secret" visits.

She tightened her veil and folded the soft cloak still more closely round her, as she stood peering there, fearing to stumble on the narrow stairway. Veronica seldom stepped down to this courtyard but it was understood that the small court, though bordering on the lower officials' quarters, was her especial corner.

She wondered, by what misunderstanding, the soldiers had not been cleared from it. She was stopped in the doorway by Fabius, who just recognised her. It appeared that in the inner-court room, there was a kind of tumult.

It all, Fabius motioned toward him, was on account of this man. Fabius added, he himself was seeing to the matter. The soldiers should escort the prisoner instantly across the strip of pavement into an inner barracks. Some sort of rough punishment (a sort of soldiers' joke) was about to be perpetrated. Veronica asked, "Need it be—perpetrated?"

Fabius begged her to step inside. Veronica said, "It isn't, as far as I can see, a joke. Where are the palace servants?" Fabius motioned to the leader of the guard but Veronica interceded. The soldiers went on, apparently preparing the stage for their little frolic. "What has this—prisoner done?"

It was difficult to know exactly what he had done, Fabius said. It had all come about by a sort of misunderstanding. Even Pilate himself was puzzled.

A phrase of Mnevis, repeated, strangely, just this afternoon, returned signally to jar her, striking a key note of related memory. Mnevis had told Veronica she was malign and terrible. The phrase resounded somewhere, struck some answering bell note. Something malign and terrible was at work here. The man, she noted, was absolutely worn out.

"But Nobilior—what then, is it?" Nobilior repeated that none of them could find out. It was a certain festival, occasion demanded the freeing of a prisoner. An old scamp (held in bonds for just this specific reason) had been freed in the courtroom. The ceremonial was a usual spring-festival, a trivial parody of Justice, that Pilate supported, for reasons of diplomacy.

Pilate, Nobilior repeated, had used his amazing powers of logic, put forward his argument, but it hadn't helped things.

The Jewish priests had refused the official robber and way-laid this man, no one knew why; he had been dragged forcibly to the throne-room. There was some clamour. Pilate wasn't about to judge an innocent man guilty without a show of trial. A few paid hirelings jeered and there was back-talk from their circle about blasphemy, this fellow making himself out one with their Almighty.

There were, Veronica noted, beads of sweat upon the fore-head of Nobilior. "It's a hell of a bore and an excruciating tangle. If we let this man go, the claque, hired by the inner priestcraft, is going to break into some sort of uproar. If Pilate signally puts them down through the imperial body-guard, there is going to be uproar of no mean significance, and possibly an outbreak from these very returned mercenaries, he has so long been suspecting."

This man, Nobilior repeated (he himself held) was no Jew, his aspect resembled more that of certain of the new Mithraic priesthood. He was more like that anyhow, from the little he could judge from talking with his fellows, argu-ing of Light, of Darkness, or an Eternal Father, the exact replica of the Mithraic trinity, with its Star, Shepherds chanting and Angels (an Eastern symbol), its cup and lilies and communion of brotherhood in the caves.

Veronica stepped nearer. She saw a young face, bearded in the manner of certain of the Eastern devotees. She realised with a shock of recognition that it was the face of her little sun-god. "Is it true then? Have you been taken falsely?" The man bent his head, whether in affirmation or despair or pride, Veronica didn't know. Nobilior said, "There's no use speaking to him. Pilate has been asking every sort of question with the subtlety of the viper. He wanted to show quite, quite clearly to the hired claque, to the ignoble and blood-thirsty partisans of the inner synagogue, that the man was innocent. Pilate was Socratic, playing into the hand of this man; so even a bowed head, or a hand raised, would have put the thing right. But he wouldn't bow or signal anything. He just stood there." Veronica looked closer. Indeed, he just stood there.

Aeons might pass and he would still be standing—just there. That, Veronica apprehended. She turned now to Nobilior, "Can't you punish your underlings, you the full body-officer of Pilate? In the name of Tiberius?"

Tiberius—the name sounded odd to Fabius in this space of shadowed courtyard. Tiberius? What did Tiberius stand for?

"Here we are, not one of us, with all our power and authority, of any use whatsoever. The mob had only to shout Caesar, and Pilate with all his autocracy was baffled. 'You will bring offense to Caesar,' they said." Well, Pontius well knew he would. Fabius forewarned Veronica. "Pilate is cursing in the ante-chamber." Veronica said, "I'll go there to him."

Veronica found Pilate. He was not accustomed to this sort of interruption. He was standing by the window, himself facing the same square. Apparently, he hadn't seen her—or having seen her, did not recognise her. The scraping of the chair, the rasp of her sandal (she purposely brushed against it) brought Pilate swinging round. His shoulders were hunched forward, like a professional gladiator, his head set heavy, his chin out-thrust. He said, "O—you Veronica?"

She said, "So odd? Oh, most august." He felt she was jeer-ing at him. "At this moment, in my—office?" She said, "Yes, but there's singular disturbance in my courtyard, just outside the window. It isn't usual either." He said, "There's been minor civic rioting all day. How did you come to miss it?" Veronica said, "I was with a—friend. The usual sort of mission." Though usually indifferent, Pilate seemed to await further explanation. It was not his custom to inquire of his wife's visits. She supposed she had annoyed him, coming here. Veronica continued.

"I was out this afternoon, came back, veiled as is usual. I went to a shrine of Isis." She was not lying to him. It occured to Veronica suddenly that her visits to Mnevis *were* by way of searching for a feminine counter-part of deity, though Mnevis couldn't be associated actually with Aphrodite. "At least," she found oddly that she wanted to get the thing straight, "I went to a woman who is a Cretan—well, a sort of priestess." Pilate was frowning at her or rather frowning at the curtain opposite. It seemed the guard was about to enter. There was scuffling, feet of mail; silence.

Further, Veronica heard vague, muttered words, having to do with enemies of Caesar.

"Who are these enemies," she asked, "these enemies of Caesar?"

VIII

PILATE DID NOT ANSWER her question, but put one to her, "What has brought you?" He moved toward the table, his hand oratorically now thumping his chest. His chin now was more that of the impassioned orator than of the gladiator.

He said, "I had a habit in the old days of using my Vera. Do you remember?" She bowed, her upper-lip drawn in. The howling at the opposite end of the long chamber, seemed to reverberate almost physically, the heavy curtain swayed a little inward, as if moved actually by this buffeting of voices. There was, she saw now, need of that gladiatorial sternness.

"Well, what shall we do about it?" Veronica said, "I tell you honestly, Pontius, I was with the Cretan priestess. She had told me of a Prophet."

She stood now facing Pilate, "Is this man that Prophet?"

Pilate said, "There are many mystery-mongers"—the phrase was a common one among them—"and priests and healers, and magnetic-healers, and diverse sorts of preachers. Yes, I do think they say that he claims to be a sort of Prophet."

Veronica said, "Your very subtle policy has been, has it not, to ignore soothsayers, religious differences, any sort of religious contention here in your sanctum of Justice?"

Pilate said, "You have heard my opinion on these matters, on more than one occasion. But this time, the Jewish priesthood are trying to persuade me that there *is* a sort of inner brotherhood or circle. The man has spoken openly of prayer in secret, of a secret eye, a King or Father in secret. There has always been something secret. He speaks, it is also rumoured, to his followers in a sort of code. He says one thing that obviously, means another. He has openly admitted, on more than one occasion, that his words hold different meanings. How do I know that the kingdom he preaches, is not a sort of direct intimation that they intend setting up fortresses here or in the Islands?"

Veronica said, "You have not seen the man, then," knowing perfectly well that Pontius Pilate had been lately talking to him.

Pilate answered, "I have not only seen him but have stood him upright, like an officiating high-priest or a sort of actor. I made a stage or amphitheatre out of the very sacred circle of the August throne of judgment. I said to them repeatedly and with sufficient gesture and implication: 'see this man you have brought me.'"

Ecce homo, he repeated and *ecce homo* seemed again to resound across billowing purple-space of curtain, as answer to the argument that persisted, in the outer hallway. Veronica perceived, not for the first time, that her husband had this rare histrionic gift of presentation.

"Well, you can't—" said Veronica, indicating the in-billowing of the curtain. "Can't what?" questioned the august husband. "Why—*that* precisely," she said. It was obvious, in all conscience, what "that" meant. It rose, it shook the heavy folds of the imperial purple. It seemed to jab through and at them. Veronica drew shuddering, toward the window. She stopped. She could not look out. What had the "little joke" turned into now? She returned to the table. Her husband still stood there, oratorical, forensic, gladiatorial, his mind and his sense acute, perceptive, yet arrogantly determined not to give in. "I can't give in to this mob."

Pilate, it appeared, was thinking of his own pride; check-mated, Pontius Pilate was considering not that Jew outside, but his own predicament. Someone, somehow had caught him. Astute in mental abstraction, their religion could be tabulated in terms of measure and weight, the lingo of the counting-house; and one of the Hebraic inner priesthood, had so trapped him.

"Well—when Jew meets—when Greek meets—when Jew meets *Rome,* Veronica, what is there to do about it?"

"There is no choice," answered Veronica, "you certainly can't give up this innocent victim. You can't—" she shuddered, facing him now, herself imperial, "*crucify* him."

The roar from behind dividing purple was no longer prolonged as a storm or distant waters that might, mercifully, for just a moment, die down. There was nothing any more, impersonal about it. It was one voice, one personal and fiery invective. It repeated, "You are no friend of Caesar's"—stage-set, planned chorus and counter-chorus, the second party repeated hideous rote, rhythmic invective. Their "crucify him, crucify him" meant more than just kill, banish, send into exile. It was not a cry of any human passion, but such as people had uttered before when roused to frenzy before the crowded Capitol; war-hysteria against whatever province at the moment was out of favour. "Crucify him" was a cry to war, having nothing to do with any set of people; war-madness, war-hysteria. Veronica saw that it was war-hysteria.

"You mean—?"

"I mean," said Pilate to her, "if I do or don't do this, I am equally in a bad position. I mean that war in any form will be violently opposed by authorities at the Capitol. I was sent here, as you well know, for subtle policies. You know pro and con of every conceivable religious problem has been worn thread-bare. At Rome—how will Tiberius discriminate? Already there have been violent rumours and invidious incriminations. Not so much against this Jew and Jewry (this particular iconoclast), but against the inner doctrine of the returned mercenaries and their cave-worship. I had thought Fabius might unravel some of the mysteries, and get the thing smoked out. 'Smoke them out,' I said to Fabius, 'like wasps in a tree-hollow.' Fabius found the wasps were honeybees and their honey, opium."

"Fabius?"

"I have long been tracking and trying to stabilise this same matter. Fabius Nobilior is certainly one of the converts to this cult of Mithra."

Mithra. Veronica recalled her former talk with Fabius; Mithra was the enemy of darkness. "There is no harm in Mithra."

"And you might equally infer there is no harm in this man."

"What harm then is there?"

"There is no harm in either," Pilate answered; "the harm," he swung out his right arm in that decisive professional gesture toward the curtain, "is in the people."

"But the people—with a just and upright ruler?"

"Find me your upright ruler."

"Pilate—yourself."

His shoulders shook ironically; the familiar aspect of his indrawn lower lip took, to Veronica, monstrous dimension. Pilate seemed to have been caught invidiously snarling, probably sensing one of his most virulent enemies at work here.

She repeated, "You can't crucify him."

"I never said I would. The thing is to get the man free—yet

with some semblance of conniving with authority." Pontius Pilate repeated, "We must get the man free."

"Surely that's quite a simple matter."

Pilate scowled at her, "No—how can we? There is only one way, Veronica. You know, perfectly, the people. They must have their little side-show. You know perfectly the people, Veronica."

"You mean," she jumped astutely to his logic, "that you will disguise the prisoner?"

She knew that was done. Distinguished political offenders, doomed to unseemly exile in the distant Egyptian turquoise or the Brittanic tin-mines, were often bought off, a criminal offender tricked up, substituted. "You mean—"

"You know yourself, Veronica, there's nobody like him, to fake his astute iconoclastic manner. No, we must take the more difficult measure. We must actually nail him up there—"

"Impossible—"

"With Rome," answered Pilate dryly, "all things are possible."

Pilate's wife was—enervated with this Pilate. His malign judgment, as he explained the matter, unnerved her. He said he understood men and the mob; explaining subsidiary matters, said frankly they could do it. Veronica re-asserted there was no way. Pilate repeated, "There is that one." Veronica sank down on the low stoool, her head swimming, there was shouting both sides, fresh invective from the open window. "Well, there *is* this one chance."

"Then I am to go to—"

"Go to any of your circle. There's no time for me. I can't possibly leave the throne-room."

Veronica said, "Suppose this—drug doesn't work?"

Pilate said, "At least, he will die unconscious."

Veronica said, "I don't believe you, Pilate. Anyway, what would happen—"

"Happen?"

"If they found out."

"Veronica," said Pontius Pilate, "a Roman has no option. I have resources if I am discovered and condemned for negligence of duty. It is for this prisoner, I suffer. His law does not sanction the aristocratic gesture, his creed is one of outward denial; the reed in the river, the wild-bird on the wing, the field-blossom all hold one law for him. To him, all things are beautiful. The bird on the wing—" He paused there.

Veronica was puzzled. "Where have you heard this?"

"There are informers; these religions, sometimes my business, are occasionally my past-time."

"You never told me of it."

"You had your own way of searching. What is left to the civilised world but a new pulse of searching? The old gods are worn out, the new gods are not yet established. I have sought as others, among the fashionable of Capitoline circles."

"I thought you were above superstition, Pilate."

"I trust Veronica, I have been. I knew there was danger in the cult of Mithra. But this man being an isolated poet, I meant to spare him. His people have not been unconversant with me."

"Who first—if I may ask?"

"I think the first who brought him to my knowledge was Memnonius."

"Memnonius?" Veronica facing Pontius, formed definite conclusion, "I have it." Pilate did not deem it worthwhile to ask her "what," as a guard swung back the curtain. He motioned imperiously to Veronica who still paused, half hidden in the drawn fold.

"Then if I see Memnonius, if I find some sort of—opiate?"

Pilate motioned her away from the outer crowded throne-room. "Anything."

Veronica knew his "anything" was final.

Memnonius was not far. He had never been far. It appeared this action was one of singular significance to everyone. If Pilate condemned the prisoner, then he himself was de-meaned in spirit. If he forgave him without sanction of the holiday-making people, then he was condemned by them and by Tiberius. It was evident anyhow, that the prisoner was a marked man. Let him escape on a ship, concealed among bales of linen, wool, from or to Egypt, from or to the capital. What was there for him? Political prisoners had a way of shrinking to singular insignificance. Memnonius was drawing Veronica along the crowded hall-way; jeers presently were si-lenced. Pilate perhaps, had momentarily found a way out.

"Listen, Memnonius, I must have something. There is a prisoner—" She knew there was no need to elucidate. Mem-nonius must help her, and she must help Memnonius. The prisoner was past their helping.

"Listen—you used to speak of—buds infolded. I have been, always. I never knew anything of myself until just—this in-stant. Until just a half-hour or a few minutes since. I passed him in the court-yard."

Memnonius was silent. "Must he then perish?" she asked. Memnonius was now back in her room. He did not answer.

"Pilate says—if I can—if we can—we must try to save him."

Memnonius answered, "Well spoken for a Roman." Veronica felt the jeer there. "Does Pilate consider ever, that there are codes, different ways of facing death? To a Roman of aristocratic circles, suicide is a solution. It is not, to certain of the inner priesthood. How could we offer him an opiate? To begin with, he wouldn't take it." "There are certainly ways of insisting." "Not with his sort." Pilate was staunch really, she sided now with Pilate.

"Surely you see that Rome is seeking to adjust the balance? Where but in Rome is Justice so singularly manifest?"

"Justice," sneered Memnonius. "Is there one god then? The only Roman contribution to the code of living, to the march-forward of what you call civilization, is a few roads and Justice by name."

"You wrong us—I am unhappy. Pilate loves him."

"What has Pilate ever loved but his own self, his own wit and power to tell the truth? But lately in the throne-room, he quips, 'What is Truth, precisely?'" "Truth—that was—" she murmured. "It was a name he called me, Vera. If Pilate asked you or the assembly, what is truth, he meant Vera-ikon. Help me, Memnonius."

She felt at home in her own room. The Egyptian was faulty, she saw now, the Egyptian was blind. He would not accept their yearning toward something else. He had an occult code; as it applied to men and manifest Justice, it was somewhere lacking. Why should this man die? "Why should you let him die, Memnonius?"

"There are codes, creeds, there are many forms of dying."

"I know that—but this man—" *Ecce homo* resounded as if from distant battle-trumpets. *Ecce homo.* In him was manifest, she had just seen, her own Etruscan sun-god; Fabius perhaps sensed in him some occult Mithra. Ah Fabius! There was yet Fabius.

"Memnonius, long ago you loved me. You said often I was a bud infolded. You said you would give anything to see me ray-out, my buds unfolding. Memnonius, no amount of physical ecstasy has given what he gave me. Help me to save this Jew of the Etruscans, this Jew of the Greeks, this Jew of the Egyptians."

Memnonius answered, "You can not, I tell you, save him."

"Then help me," Veronica argued, "to save myself. Give me the opiate that you used to speak of. Give me some form of numbness." She flung herself face downward. "Give me some sort of hope—to numb my senses—let me die even."

Memnonius carried the phial with him, she knew that. He had often spoken to her of a secret danger, a threat that he must stand armed to cope with. He had once proffered her this very phial. Now, she held it in her cold hand. It was the very sealed flask he had once offered her, at the time of that hideous outbreak of plague in the lower city.

Veronica felt that the scene just now so dramatically enacted, had not been performed by her. It was not Veronica who had thrown herself down on this same couch, still rumpled with uneven covers and scattered pillows. All this drama, had taken place perhaps in a single half-hour, maybe in less time. She had gone to a window, had looked out, had walked like one in a trance downstairs. She had crossed a courtyard into a forbidden sanctum, that of her Roman husband. All that had happened in less time than it takes to tell it and now, in her hand, was the answer to the whole thing. One moment, and she would again rise, would again wonder at the force that urged her on, would again be unastonished to find herself speaking strange yet familiar words, as in a play.

The whole thing was put in order, as if rehearsed by Fabius, by Pilate, by Veronica. A sort of central figure was the reason for this drama, he would be standing on that stage—the central figure, but having little to do with the entrances and exits of actors, speaking almost no word, set there like a statue in a Greek drama before a gate-way or on an altar in a temple precinct. He was the *Deus* who steps down, makes his solemn speech after the play is over. The play was already under way—was over. But she must find Fabius.

"I couldn't stop them." "It's all right." Veronica knew that she would find him just there, standing like a Roman in a drama, his right hand upraised, his other hand clenched and hanging by his left side.

Veronica touched his shoulder. "I did all that I could with Pilate. Pilate says we may yet save him."

"Pilate himself," questioned Nobilior, "gave his consent to this thing?"

The mob-howls and muffled thuds as of the lash on raw flesh, meant just nothing to Veronica herself, who felt mercifully numbed. She realised that nothing could be done now, unless the prisoner himself consented.

"When—it—is—over—take him a bowl of water. Pretend to revive him as if for further beating. Let the men think that you must save him for the final torture."

Fabius said, "It has occurred to me that if they put the whip-thong hard enough—he might—he might possibly die without it."

"No," said Veronica, "how little you know people. The people have been howling out their blood-lust. They must have the very embodiment of anguish. They want to *see* him dying in agonies of torture. They want terribly to see it."

Fabius, facing the wide eyes of his former mistress, thought for a stark second, she had gone mad.

"Put this thing in cool water. It is colorless—see that the prisoner drinks it."

"He won't take any sort of opiate."

"I know that—he will be too exhausted, he won't think—for once, he won't think." Automatically, Fabius took the phial from her.

It was noxious, she knew, a compound of colourless poppy-juice and some unnamed, secret remedy. So profound was her trust in Memnonius and his judgement, that in the past, she had never sought this of him. The temptation to negate existence might be too great.

She had discussed the popular subject of suicide with him often. The strict etiquette of the Roman superiors demanded not only a superficial knowledge of these things, but a specific attitude as well. The sharp knife-edge (kept particularly whetted for this matter, on many a dressing-table) was of course the most accepted, the gentleman's usual method. The hot bath and the razor-blade didn't always appeal. It might prove a little awkward—a hot bath might cause comment, at just the required moment. Veronica had, in the old days, spoken openly of all this to Memnonius.

All knowledge has its own sphere, its own little shelf or numbered box or scroll pushed sidewise on it; knowledge is put away, closed or rolled under, like a precious half-forgotten parchment. Occasion arises and it is there, just as forgotten javelin-practice may hold in good stead, in sudden emergency. All that had happened in these past few minutes, Veronica felt was pre-ordained; she herself lost sight of the spectacle, was slightly bored by the progress of it. It was bound to happen, so it would happen. "What must be, must be." Veronica realised now, in an emergency, she was adopting first the code of Memnonius, second that of the Roman Empire, third ... some not yet quite definite kind of emotional ritual. She knew however her last, or first, reason for so acting was simply that she loved this manifestation of her old gods; the young man was beautiful.

Not perhaps in the accepted Roman mannner; he was too slight, not robust enough, his head, drooping forward, was that of some early half-god, some Ionian or perhaps some later, more skilfully defined Etruscan ... that curious sort of calculating aspect. The man was, of course, a Jew. He had, it appeared now, on careful consideration, mapped out his spiritual affinities, made the whole of the art of loving and appreciation of God, of Nature applicable in merely human terms, symbols easily grasped by all. He had his counter, as it were—his coin for each thing, his measure of wheat, the cubit —the weights and measures were constantly elaborated in his speech. Speech that Mnevis had astutely outlined, returned, renewing her vigor.

Veronica, seeking Fabius for the last time in the outer door-way, said "Now let the show continue." She was herself so rapt, so poignantly in danger that she did not care what happened. All that mattered was Nobilior should proffer a goblet to lips, parched and trembling in the final agonies.

The man, half fainting, quaffed the proffered liquid.

IX

THIS VERY MAN and his courteous definition of man's ultimate dignity had been sent, it seemed, to differentiate between the literates and the ungodly. There was a code that pertained, that held. Pilate was a gentleman, a Roman. He had made his effort, had accepted incalculable chance of degradation by even so much as hinting to his wife—his supposed infallible partner—that there was a solution other than the obvious brute one.

Pilate might have flung his assurance and his imperial authority into the faces of the Jewish rulers. He had refrained from that. Pilate in that, had proved beyond doubt his own autocracy, his right to respect the spiritual, as well as his mere imperial acclaim. Pilate had let himself be considered beaten by the mob. They had seen through his game, however. It was formidable stale-mate. Pilate would have secret satisfaction, however, knowing that the death of this Prophet was only symbolic, a way of propitiating mob-clamour. The mob demanded its circus spectacle; just as in early ceremonies Memnonius had described for her, the Egyptian people, not initiate to the inner mysteries, must themselves believe that Osiris was torn fragment from fragment, limb horribly from limb. The father of Osiris was supposed to have hallowed the mutilation. This, however, was simply the outer reading. No mythical "father" could by any exaggeration be held responsible. The mob, the populace, the people had condemned him.

Veronica waiting in a dark room, knew in some specific

corner of her odd consciousness that this very small event held in some way, the whole germ of all doctrinaire philosophy. One teacher was just like any other. The *grain of mustard seed,* the *seed cast into the ground* was an Eleusinian precept. This was no new doctrine really. The novelty was bringing that precept into line with every-day existence. This man in that was as great as Osiris, greater than the Hellenic sun-god. Yet for all that, he *was* Osiris, *was* the Hellenic sun-god, demonstrably in beauty and in wisdom. It was true then—as he had predicted, noticeably—in his own case. Here lay intrinsic wisdom: that men are gods. What he was, he constantly asserted, all men were. All men and (this was the oddest thing about it) all women. What Eastern prophet had ever given women a place in the spiritual hierarchy? The Greek certainly, but then the Greek, Veronica knew, had merely sublimated and intellectualised the old set of symbols.

This Jew seemed to combine the Greek way and an occult wisdom in a curious precise manner. His *consider the lilies* linked his cult of nature with the old shrines—where lilies always floated before the feet of the blue-robed Isis. (The lilies were the flower, notoriously, of Isis.) His talk of birds, of doves, noticeably again brought dove-worship into human consciousness; every tree had its own fruit, he asserted. The fruit of the tree and the vine made him one with the Eleusinian Dionysus. *Greater love has no man,* however, was his first creed.

Love, it was evident, had its own advantages—and disadvantages. Take love, in this instance. Love had incarnated Veronica into Veronica. This Vera, Vera-ikon—whom Pilate had long since said had an odd knack for forensic rectitude—was not the Vera, Vera-ikon that sat here. Love propelled one forward, dragged backward, made a sort of whirl-pool. Love, it was obvious, for all of Plato and his argument, had no logic. Love projected forward so that closed eyes, blinded with an odd sort of not-seeing, saw more clearly: a long road, the dust of countless feet, the light of that dull half-day reflected from hammered breast-plates.

There was a wind rising. It tossed a screen or awning about, flip-flap, from one of the upper windows. Veronica felt she was in some old house, dead in the centre of eternal death and stillness.

There was the usual rumble of passing chariots, the shout as some servant or gardener called to another across terraces, to hurry within doors some of the more exotic fragile rose-trees. (Veronica thought the thing must now be over.) Rose-trees would be placed in palace arcades, or set before ornate capitols. The wind would continue to flap an odd bit of canvas that was the careless witness to some servant's negligence. It seemed to Veronica that the whole world was stamping through churned-up white dust, horribly, toward that stark hill. Servants, masters, soldiery, the cosmopolitan rabble that was this town, Jerusalem. She exaggerated, she knew. The punishment, in this instance, was only that meted to a common political offender. Fabius Nobilior, she remembered, was with them.

She held on to that: Fabius is with them. Nobilior might come back, clank heavy arms, make the palace breathe again. She saw the palace in ruins: it lay heavy, lizards ran in and out of broken crevices. The old palace had no rose-trees, no flap even of a torn bit of cloth, no tapestries, no candles set stark and glowing, nor any live torch. The palace was in ruins—half of it worn off, gnawed by countless weathers; in and out of crevices, snails crawled, one snail had eaten away a half of a dock-leaf—no lilies anywhere. The palace was dead, lost in stubble, sheep-pens, tents, a row of crumbling houses. The palace would house the ass and the wild-sheep, the goat would sniff at the fallen water-basin. The palace would stand, objective re-incarnation; not Rome–not Rome–Pilate was standing by her.

Veronica's eyes opened wide on accustomed grandeur. Rumbling and white slash told finally, the storm had broken. Pilate remarked, "I suppose Nobilior set the thing in order?"

Veronica answered, "Not Nobilior, it was ordained that the prisoner should not die, hung up like any criminal."

Pilate said, "Has Nobilior returned, then?"

Veronica said, "I have not see him." She considered Pilate closely, said then, "Why do you ask, Pontius Pilate?"

Pontius Pilate answered, "They have sent already. I affected surprise. I said they might have the body." Veronica rose. Now was her time for action.

Action already put in motion, greets its own counter-action. Action pre-ordained, put in order, needs no self-conscious plan or plot of counter-action. She had bidden good-bye to Pilate. Nobilior, a little whiter than the livid lightning from outside, said, "We are now in our greatest danger."

There had been an earthquake. Certain of the old buildings were tottering. It was patently dangerous for Veronica to accompany him, but she insisted. She said there was no harm now; he had not died, hung there like any criminal.

Fabius said, "Nobody took much notice. The soldiers were too busy and too sated after their private escapade to pay much attention to him. He dragged the ponderous weight of his own cross. We whipped up the crowd to protestation of delight so that the man's actual condition would not be duly noted. He dragged along, already half-dead. He was utterly exhausted."

Veronica said, "Then he is—?"

"We don't know yet. We got one of his own followers, a well-to-do merchant of Arimathaea, to claim the body. We got the thing down; storm scattered the waiting people. They had scattered anyhow, most of them, some time past. They did not get any particular satisfaction from the white body that hung there, numb almost from the beginning. The writhings and imprecations of the other two, the common criminals, didn't excite them either. They had seen that sight too often. Some lingered, cheated of psychic demonstration."

"Was there any—patent demonstration from his—people?"

"—there was no demonstration. As I said, the storm came, mercifully."

She laboured that he who had healed pain might have pain taken from him. The young man lay stretched on a slab of rock. Veronica and Fabius had returned to an inner cavern. It was sealed from the outside, and a guard was set about it. Certain of the Jews had not been altogether convinced as to the prisoner's way of dying. There was lamentably little of the usual spectacle; the dignity of the pendant figure had caused not a little comment.

Fabius assured Veronica, in the half-tones they had adopted, that in the storm and the rumbling of the earthquake (these events were not infrequent, this time of the year), the people had indeed scattered. The common rabble had run off home, to roll up awnings, to salvage what the wind left of flapping tent-cloth, to bind fast doors and shutters.

Love, it appears, has its advantages. One thing is that the hand, sweeping over and through stained linen, knows automatically where to touch, where to refrain from touching. A group of Fabius' personal body-servants had accompanied them here, after the relegation of the apparently dead body to this new cave or sepulchre. The cave gave onto a passage from the rear, well hidden save to the initiate. It was, in fact, connected with the honeycomb of caves where but recently Fabius had first hailed Light as Light and rejected Dark as Darkness. It seemed fitting to Veronica that the astute young Prophet should be laid there, sleeping in the very recesses of one of the caves of Mithra.

Spices, left by a few of the frantic, though self-controlled, women of his following, lay against the stone-wall in their little boxes. Nobilior had explained how his particular danger rested with these women, who insisted on staying with him. He had recalled old ritual, Jewish liturgy, spoken to one of them in rough Aramaic, persuaded her that as it was their holy-day or Sabbath, it would be more fitting to leave the jars of incense. He would see to it that the following day—it was now almost dawn—the ladies should be admitted, and allowed to prepare the body for its burial.

Those little jars ranged along the wall, so much spice and incense, wafted perfume to the body of this Image. The Image lay as if asleep, his gesture, one clenched hand resting on the half-bared breast, alone gave proof to the unparalleled event of the turgid and overcrowded afternoon. The rain that had swept upon the ceremonial of the Crucifixion, had now ceased. Day was not far off, a crack in the stones showed a ring of light, the faintest light that warned Veronica that in a moment, they must dim the torches.

The soldiers sleeping outside had made little, if any movement; no clang of metal, silence. The men were tired out, had had some dispute with certain of the more distant and discreet of this man's followers. The whole matter had required superhuman tact on the part of the officials, and discretion from the leading officer. That man was seated to the left of the dark door-way. He was twisting hyacinth and wild myrtle-stems, wet stems of wild narcissus, flowers he had curiously pilfered in their progress through the wet field, leading to this ledge.

Formal Latin was recalled in this small chamber. Their half-whispered utterance reminded Veronica of other more special occasions. Nobilior had tended to liken her to a pear-branch in blossom, the *Meliboe pirus,* the *roscida mala,* the (to be precise) *purpureo narcisso.* All these words muttered as to some latent deity had fallen from the lips of Fabius Nobilior. They took new meaning in the little chamber. Here Veronica and Nobilior were cleansed of their own affliction. They were in love with something, Nobilior with an idea or ideal, Veronica with an actual figure. Chafing his thin hands, she perceived the Image waking. She was frightened. She turned to Nobilior. "I don't think he'll want to see me."

She sensed herself, somehow, outside this thing. The man was a young priest, of rigid discipline. He would open his eyes, be astonished at the presence of a Roman lady. This trite idea weighed heavily on Veronica.

"You must be alone, explain to him. Rub more balm on his temples. I'm going back to have restoratives, wine, fruit sent here. You yourself can't wait here, famishing."

Veronica let the hand fall on the bare breast; did not wait to see if the heavily ringed eyes would open.

X

"GREATER LOVE," said Veronica. She stiffened herself to this thing. Love was applicable to Pilate, to their early marriage, only in so far as love had made her a Capitoline lady. Love in that instance had fused her to a brother, father, a "gentleman of position," shawls with fringes and her first imperial purple. Love, without this, would have seemed unfeasible to Veronica, as song without flute-music or a banquet without the white or red-rose. Love consisted in prolongment of reality. "I love Fabius" had answered for some time. "I love Memnonius" was really a contradiction; she had loved in him the wily play of personality, wit against wit, power against power. "I love Mnevis," probably might answer. Was loving Mnevis, all told then, this "greater love"?

A peasant-girl stopped to inquire what might have been the tumult last night in the valley. The servant responded harshly, there had been a criminal indictment. The peasant stepped aside; a bearer signalled that a lady was kept waiting. It was on the slope of this particular vine-clad hill that Veronica, at Fabius' suggestion, had ordered her litter to wait for her.

The girl drew off in fright. It was common knowledge that ladies, discovered at secret trysts, had often ordered the discoverer to be—silenced.

The litter was lowered, the servants stood there waiting. Into a luminous Eastern morning-sky, a bird flew with strident song as of crystal against silver. There seemed to be a whirr, as of long-drawn insistence of metal against metal. Veronica could imagine no apt image to express her sentience at that moment. She was withdrawn from her senses, fused to this innate power of understanding. "Yet," she protested, "if the young man were not beautiful, I would not be prepared to like him." The very simplicity of her thought sustained more inner worship. She was not "in love" precisely. "He lets one out," she said to herself, regarding as if for the first time in her life, a bird breaking, as it were, the very crystal of the morning with his continuous chatter. His song became intoning, rousing of other spirits. Veronica perceived that the air was filled with others, a whole crowd of like birds, foregathered to regard the sun-rise.

Veronica motioned to her bearers. They stood as litter-bearers always stood, bending a little at the head, as in apologetic submission. They did not stand, were not taught to stand, as soldiers. Soldiers were something other—Fabius. Veronica said "Fabius," recalled that he, in his way, had fused memory with being, mind with spirit. His love like hers, was filled up; he called on the Greeks to instil meaning into the threadbare Latin imagery.

Yet, Veronica realised, she owed much of her inner peace, her new-found conscious living, to those same Greeks. It seemed, as she watched the bird twist downward and then settle in a clump of reed that stood out in the fine grass, that this was the first utterly unselfconscious moment she had ever known. Sometimes (she recalled) Bes hinted at this intimate sensing that surpasses analytical understanding. She could say honestly, "consider the birds," and repeat with a questioning inflection, "Greater love?"

The words, "Greater love," brought her back to reality. There was yet the question of getting rid of this not incon-

siderable Prophet. What now to do with him? He might presumably die yet, of heart strain and weakness. Still it would
be wiser to suppose the contrary. In her usual somewhat pal-
lid tone, Veronica indicated to her bearers the preferred path.
She felt herself grown heavy, lead among purple cushions.

When she opened her eyes, they rested on familiar features.
The face was familiar. She had lost her reasoning. She recalled one other—white, a whetstone, and poignant. "O
Mnevis. Presumably, I slept the whole way. I told the bearers
to bring me straight to your door." Her voice was conversa-
tional, seemed to have had no intermediate period of re-adjustment. From a field where wild-flowers were dark blue and
ember-red and violet, a bird had beaten upward. Though to
all appearances she was perfectly herself—she had heard the
bird-wings beat in the high air (like silver and crystal envoys
announcing a belated wedding)—she realised that she was
tired. Wings do not, however one may argue, break into fire
and shed streamers at the wing-tip like one of those new fab-
ricated Asiatic angels.

Mnevis was unnverved, mal-adjusted, was not herself.
Drawing her indoors, she made room for Veronica on the
low couch. She herself should sit down, she should rest, why
did she stare so? The last time Veronica had visited this
room, she recalled, there had been similar mal-adjustment.
That had been afternoon—a hot day—yesterday? "Was it only
yesterday that I came to see you?" Mnevis strangely did not
answer, and the prolonged silence instilled Veronica with terror. She felt she might be ill, faint before delivering her message. What it was or might be, she had not the remotest

inkling. "I have come to tell you something–" Mnevis was chafing her hands. "Get me some water–Mnevis."

Water and dark bread, little cakes, oil, a flagon of sweet wine, figs in a brown dish, grapes in their leaves, these things were standing by her. The early morning sun made jagged pattern on the floor, replica of jagged pattern of vine withies outside the window. As the sun grew higher, the birds became less shrill, it was just conceivable that that stark whetstone would dissolve–a whetstone that sharpens spirits, knives. The thing was, had been, amply demonstrated. Men can, will, instil life into their dead brothers. She herself, had not been so much enlivened, as set free. A crag seemed to insinuate itself beneath Veronica's feet and she stood alone, was just about to leap off. "Mnevis–" She would say "Mnevis" over and over, a silly name that brought to mind Heliopolis. "Persepolis, Sardonopolis," Fabius had said, "what's that to me?" Heliopolis was the sun-city. "Mnevis–he must come to the sun-city." Mnevis seemed to have suffered some shock, was still shaking, she was changed as a vine-clad hill when lava follows an earthquake. Lava itself seemed to have scorched her features. Veronica perceived that Mnevis was colourless, scorched like red-ash gone silver.

It appeared (Mnevis recited her story standing) that the man was crucified. Veronica took no stand against this, wondered vaguely whom Mnevis meant by "the man." Mnevis seemed to imply with her ghastly countenance, no way in keeping with that flood of early-morning sunlight, that somewhere, somehow, Veronica could have spared this. Mnevis was unparalleled in her stupidity.

Veronica said, "I said I would help you. Can't you, for a moment, trust me? I don't, however, know how far I have succeeded." It seemed, in that moment, that she had confessed to ghastly fraud or treason.

In as grim and strained a voice as that of the other, speaking of "crucifixion," Veronica stammered weakly, "That is the worst of it—he's not dead."

Was a curse to be laid upon her? Was Memnonius right exactly? Did psychic-law demand of the giver of psychic-wisdom, one thing, one life namely? Was there some curse? Was the law before time, cruel as the god who dismembered the dead Osiris? Was the law made for all time? Had God ordained that His son must suffer; was there no possible advancement?

"Mnevis," said Veronica, staring suddenly into a room now converted into a space with four walls, where sunlight was just sunlight, where no possible manifestation of divinity could be God, "where is the cross that hung there?" Mnevis repeated, she had put the thing away, she didn't want the symbol of dead worship. Yet her search for a new symbol had obviously been baffled. "You see Mnevis, I was right." Veronica recalled her precise argument that antique symbol can never, she had insisted, go out of religious "fashion," however "religions" may change; doves, lilies, robed women, stars and such.

"We can't find a newer symbol. We must conform to the old reality. The murder of a Jew has made that possible."

Veronica saw now (there were no two ways about it) there could be no new "religion." She had come here to this singing woman, who had protected her against the superior and worldly assaults of her lover, ironically hoping otherwise. Mnevis had proclaimed a super-doctrine, and at first assay, at first remorseless revolution of the wheel of fortune, Mnevis—in whom Veronica had laid (she realised) so implicit a trust—had doubted.

How could Mnevis doubt, sensing wind and star-chart, laying numbers out on the charts, commanding them to prance, to dance, to be allied, each with some suitable affinity? 6, for instance, Veronica recalled blithely, was affiliated with Aphrodite and when Mnevis had demonstrated that 8, 8, 8, was the exact number of the god-head and applied it to the Prophet, it had seemed feasible that the number added, re-instated and infused with a new soul should be the number of Love brought down from Heaven to Earth: 3 times 8, 24, numeral verification which resolves itself (she recalled ironically) to 2 and 4, which added, become 6, Paradise, Love on Earth exactly.

Love on Earth and supreme surrender, surrender to divinity, Life accepted rather than Death condoned—had she been wrong? "Mnevis, it may be I have failed," a word that had never passed Veronica's lips, now passed them—"or sinned." What was sin exactly? Sin was bungling the affair, missing the clue.

Sin is the supreme arrogance. So she and Pontius Pilate, unwilling, at any rate to themselves, that Rome and Roman Justice should become a mockery, had permitted this: a man condemned to death by star, by star-chart, by numbers of ancient wisdom—had been set free. Memnonius was perhaps right. She, the Ambassador of Roman Justice, had cheated.

Ecstasy had overcome her, devotion to an idea, an abstraction. Whatever outwardly, men might come to think, it had been her inward boast that she and her husband were no mean emissaries, but worthily allied to Rome. Veronica now held on to something, the edge of a whirling crater.

She pulled herself out. She would not faint. "I want you to try, Mnevis, to make some sense of this. I want you to understand precisely that Rome keeps its promise." The flutter of sparrow-wings seemed a crude parody of the Imperial Eagle's greatness. Veronica saw the eagle, helpless as any sparrow. She saw the sparrow that shall in no wise fall to the ground without Eternal Knowledge of a benign Omnipotence; it spread wings, shot fire from its wingtips like some new-fangled Asiatic angel.

The Eagle and the legions; death in the Bactrian deserts. It was Fabius who had succumbed—not Veronica. "Listen, be sensible. The man is not dead. I left him with a bodyguard, this—*friend* I spoke of and some others. They were hidden at dawn in a hill-cave, one of the party had been relegated before I left to accost some peasant, find him suitable disguise, beggar or scholar-garment. Our whole idea was to bring the drugged Prophet food, wine, bread, get him on his feet, turn him out to wander. Roads are filled with beggars."

Stars may go out but Love, never. Veronica wondered that one so clearly "adept" as this Mnevis should have so little wisdom. "Don't be a fool—don't sit there shivering. I saved the man's life. Now you at least, protect it. Try to remember that he's ill and hungry."

It had been easy enough to stuff a leather-wallet with those same figs, to prepare flagon of wine, to fold a fresh napkin about the remains of the brown loaf. "I don't know—won't know, for certain (make anyhow for the sea-coast) which boat will take you, or to which island you'll be taken, Cyprus, Crete possibly. You will find your Asterios fitly upright again among field-tulips. Be at least helpful in this. I can't leave Jerusalem and—my work here. I have a diplomatic customer —one Aelius Claudius who knows everything of triremes and their sailings. He'll help you."

Veronica jerked Mnevis upright. She realised then that the woman was not stupid. She herself had been wounded, psy-chically stricken by the sight of yesterday. How much more Mnevis, Veronica conceded; Mnevis, she now realised, had not known that the figure hanging there, inert, drained of blood, wasn't really suffering. Mnevis had not had the some-what problematical satisfaction of knowing that, toward sun-down, that same body would be tactfully removed, the nails fastened so lightly to the bound wrists extracted, and a court-doctor (one of the private attendants of Nobilior) summoned to bathe, to bind up those hands. Hands raised in benedic-tion, hands that had touched foreheads beaded with death-sweat, hands that had freed parching birds from the wicker-hampers of the temple-market, hands that had summoned God to Earth quite simply with a gesture, "You are all gods, not one less capable than I am."

"Mnevis, I told you from the beginning or I tried to tell you—he's not dead."

XI

WHAT HAD SHE LOVED THEN? A stray peripatetic philosopher? That was possible. But it was not the philospher, nor even the poet that had drawn her. No. She worked the thing out, in that cold way that Pilate admired in her; that Vera, Vera-ikon, as he sometimes ironically called her, seemed a part in herself, something frozen, to which she could speak, as to a statue in a shrine. She, this wife of Pilate, was a mass of contradictions; everything surrounding that inner statue, that self, was false. Only the Vera-ikon was true. Well, Memnonius had clarified that for her, she could act always. Deep in her, was another person that had never acted. Who was that person? Veronica said, "I am Veronica."

She didn't, to be exact, seem to be anybody. She held to this preciseness, in order to convince herself who she was. It was, she thought, like putting a round stone, a heavy ball of lapis, some uneven lump of turquoise (from those mines in Egypt) in the rough, on a spread-out parchment. She was the spread-out parchment. Let the ikon hold it. And then she thought, I still have that parchment with the criss-cross of planets' names, the numbers of my own name and the map of my palm. She did not think it worthwhile to uncurl that hand, that now, she noticed, lay clenched, heavy in the softness of her dress.

The cloth was deep-red or purple, not the imperial purple, it was purple—she drew back, not naming it in her mind, not asking why it was purple, what sort of purple it was. She recognised in herself this tendency at this moment, to draw back. There was something she wanted to forget.

She wanted to remember. (Not that she would ever be in danger of not-remembering.) The thing in her mind was a jet of flame, it was a hard flame, it was the flame of a wick that, trebly plaited, was burning in a shell. There was a sort of shell in which Mnevis burnt a wick. It was stained alabaster but looked like a seashell. She remembered the sea.

They would be beating now, out in it. Of course, she could never forget that trip with Pilate from Rome—but that is not what she thought. There had been other sea-trips, off their own coast. "I am Etruscan," she said. "I am Etruscan" meant something. "I am Roman." But "I am Roman" sounded dreary to her, it was ornate, set round, prohibitive as Rome's roads and military dictates, her own husband. Pilate was generous. Why—Pilate is generous. Almost, in a moment, she wanted some reason to doubt this, she wanted to be a beggar. O, no, I would not. She thought of her bath, that shallow marble basin, and the cool-tiles of the outer rest-room. She remembered the array of onyx, alabaster, and the blue-glazed glass-jars and phials; why, there were even earth ones. Certain perfumes carried better, Arabian specialists asserted, in the native pottery of their own lands. The fragrance ... flowers. It had been odd to think that Fabius, in that tomb, had been weaving wild-flowers. Narcissus—as if he had clutched handfuls from the meadow—for death—or life. It had been a death-room and a bride-room. Who then, was bride? Mnevis? No, not Mnevis.

She tried not to think of the young man. He was beautiful but from what she had learned of him, he had a way of evading issues. There was something he evaded. Life, she supposed, exactly. Why had he wanted to die? He had reached a height of quiet eminence. Was he afraid of slipping? Better men than he, she asserted, quit life, their dictates worn threadbare, after the first excitement of novelty. Would this man's?

She didn't know. After all, he was a poet, for all his disdain of the usual implements, the scroll, ink-horn and reed. He didn't meticulously cut precepts on stone or even outline them in wax. He didn't write anything. Not that that mattered. His followers were not, as was presupposed by many, all illiterate. There were scholars among them—well, he had seen to that. His least word would not be wasted. Least word? What did she know of his word?

Why, she thought, I don't really know anything. I took certain of Mnevis' remarks to heart. Mnevis, in a fine frenzy, talked of sparrows, of lilies, and I quibbled about the lilies. I remember arguing with her one day, that the dove (*harmless as doves,* he said) was no new symbol. Mnevis knew that as well, better even than I. Crete had brought forth that cult of lilies long since. There were designs on those old parchments copied from copings and a frieze; that great palace was ruined, long since.

Men turned sideways, awkwardly, in the ridiculous convention of the temples Memnonius talked of. Memnonius and Mnevis were both old-fashioned. But Mnevis had caught on to something. She had managed to instil something of this new Prophet's certainty into her own cult of numbers, of star-maps and patterns. Mnevis specifically stated, however, that the Master, as she called him, would have nothing to do with the creed of the Asiatic star-gazers; he avoided all confusion, would not be linked with starry prophecies. But she said he had a neat trick of checking old things out with new; there was really nothing new in any of his precepts, the serpent, the scorpion, the egg. He talked of old things. As a matter of fact, he couldn't get away from them. Now Fabius—she remembered Fabius.

Fabius had outlined a doctrine of absolute originality. That cave-worship, of course, was old; but the candles, the communion, the wafer stamped with the cross, the pontifical solemnity, yet simplicity, of that Mithraic offering of a young bull, held something unique. That actual blood-sacrifice was as old as any ritualistic act, yet Veronica sensed something subtly spiritual in that gathering of war-wearied veterans worshipping a young god.

Mnevis had been tired out. The young Jew had been reckless. His followers had no sense of organisation, had scattered at the instant crack of thunder and the earthquake. (True, one of them had come immediately to Pilate for the body, but it was Fabius, partly, who had stage-managed that.) She herself had managed Fabius—so, taken all in all, there was nothing that his followers had done to save him. Pilate had done his best. Well, Pilate—

She wouldn't think about Pilate, wouldn't think at all of the matter. Because—there was something, she believed, that she could tell no one. Her hand rose, clenched, fell, rose again. She found herself beating time, as it were, to the throb of galleys. She felt herself urging the oars of that boat, speaking as if to her own tense heart, beat fast, beat fast, beat faster. Yet who would think of following that inconspicuous trader (making, as Claudius had promised, for Cyprus or Crete), or search in bundles of undistinguished linen, bales of unspun cotton, for more precious matter? Claudius saw to it, it wasn't the sort of boat that sea-robbers follow. They had been gone now two days.

She said, "They have been gone now two days." Soon, wind and weather being propitious, they should touch Cyprus. Would he visit in Cyprus, the famous temple of Aphrodite? No. Mnevis had insisted that he was not interested in that sort of magic. He was a physician, he was a poet, the son of God, but then he would spoil this, by saying that we are all equally—equal in capacity—sons of that God. That Father. Veronica thought backward. Her mind seemed to spin in an abyss, like an insect over a smoking oil-lamp's noxious fumes. She would be lost. There was something that seized her, she would be whirled into an abyss—*he who loseth his life*—

—*shall save it,* she added after a moment of suffocating blankness. A dark cloth seemed to pass over the luminous surface of her mind. Yes, she supposed she was wrong. She would never catch on, like Mnevis. She had no answer; but had she waited for one? Well, she had not given him the chance to answer. She had not waited in that cool, empty rock-cavern for an answer.

She had not waited for his thanks.

His thanks? Would he thank her?

His thanks? He had wanted death and she had dragged him from it. He had wanted final consummation, union with the ultimate, with the parent, the father, his father. (Why not his mother? It would be more natural to think of death, the peaceful darkness, as one's mother. Perhaps he had made it impossible any more, for anyone to visualise the mother—

Demeter. There was Aphrodite, the young, the forever smiling; there was Hera, virgin, always the exquisite bride.) Jesus
had not meant Zeus by that father. Yet how could he mean
any other? Was he Zeus? Saturn, Zeus' father, was more like
the Jews' jealous tribal-god, with his prohibitive list of shalt-
nots. This new son was not so moral. He sat with song-girls,
any sort of prostitute was welcome at his feasts. Saturn would
not have had that; the sacred fragments of papyrus she had
read with Memnonius were witness to it; and others, less familiar (she had had certain of Pilate's scribes search for her)
insisted on this same rigorous ethic. But then, Memnonius
explained, Jove or Jehovah had had to hold his dwindling
tribe together. The Greeks ethically were fluid, too fluid—
were lost. The Greeks had suffered, been dispersed like her
own Etruscans.

Jehovah was a policeman, not that the world didn't need a
policeman. Tiberius, in Rome, had set up a similar sort of effigy; his Capitoline Jupiter was without imagination. This Jesus dared put forward a new axiom: God has imagination. He
insisted that God, though he had the eye of the eagle (that
bird of Jupiter), yet had the tenderness of the dove, or even the
common domestic fowl who fluffs out her feathers, to collect
her chicks. He stripped off the outer shell of the soul. Veronica herself was now as defenseless as a new-hatched chick;
why, all this, she thought, was my egg-shell! She regarded the
agate and cornelian and lazuli objects strewn about her, as a
builder of a dam sees across a seething river that the dam has
broken. Her mind swung between grandiose and simple images. He made one see things like that. The whole of her existence had been built up on a falsehood.

But there was life—everywhere. That's just what he said.
Why even here—here, there is life. I have made life. Her soul

swelled in painful disproportion. If he is like Zeus, then I am –I am–... Almost by some trick of her perception, she thought of herself as the creator of this being, who was yet as her young father.

He had created her. For a moment, she had escaped–if only for a moment.

Now that Fabius stood there, she knew she had been waiting too long. She had been waiting for two days, neurotically on edge. She couldn't go on like this. Now she knew she must get back, get right into her body or else wing out forever. Before speaking, here was that infinitesimal moment of hesitation, or psychic re-adjustment.

"Well–Fabius?"

He said that she looked pale, was she ill?

"No–only waiting."

"Well, I have come back."

With a start, she realised that he thought she was waiting for him. How make that clear? But had she been waiting for him? In the curious state of half-life in which she had been wandering, there were no barriers, all men were one in that spiritual kingdom, there were no social definitions. If she were one with Fabius–her heart caught, stopped–she could have counted to seven. Then it plunged back to its accustomed rhythm, accompanied with what she could almost have described as, a roaring in her ears. She supposed she was very hungry. She had left word that she was not to be disturbed, except for that jar of water, periodically renewed.

"And those–others?"

Fabius might have considered it expedient to ignore her

anguish. He must know of it. It seemed to beat out from her now, in wave-lengths of silver, slightly jagged, like an Oriental's sword-blade. Then the anguish seemed to flow straight, to be straight silver rays, that flowed or rayed out, yet turned inward to defeat her. If they reached him—will they reach him? Fabius had helped her. Fabius again must help her. But Fabius, in his turn, wasn't thinking of her.

To himself, he admitted his predicament. His mind had been ready for revelation; almost as he watched the sun-rise, he had seen God. Poised for revelation, his soul had winged out. But his suave mind had caught him, and his soul could just not break that barrier. He now understood this young sooth-sayer, this scholarly, unrobed priest. There were comparatively few among his followers, Fabius thought in retrospect, who actually had understood him. For all that, this Jesus captured the intellect; the mind spun its length of thread like any spider, and on that thread, the soul—frail butterfly—fluttered, cognizant of danger. If the thread broke?

It might have broken. Fabius could have laid down his war-gear, weapons, insignia of office, on that clean strip of sand. They had broken out of a small cypress wood. The trees were stunted by sea-wind. Fabius thought of the cypress as a mountain-growing, healing, balm-tree. Those little trees, as if left as seedlings by wind, by bird, had struck unsuitable dead soil. Yet they spread aromatic scent of bark, taste of resin. It was hot in the little hollow.

Claudius had arranged the matter, the small vessel was riding at anchor, about to put in just there for water. They had travelled with the bare handful of soldiers to guard a prisoner, who needed no guard. He had slept in the carter's wagon, half covered with an old sail. The carter was not curious. He sensed, as is the way with his sort, that his single passenger was in trouble. The woman walked most of the way, by the cart.

This was the woman that Veronica had described to him. He had not spoken to her, admitting to himself that she took to the road more like a woman from a vineyard or corn-field, than the town streets. Now, he wanted desperately, as he stood by that sand, with the shallows showing green—like those aquamarines Veronica had set in a great bracelet—some answer. In her room, he had turned Veronica's bracelet to the light and the stones had showed cold depth of water. Now, seeing the very water, he thought of those stones. For him, for Veronica, he supposed, life went on, in two separate dimensions.

He had to "weigh himself down" with something. His temptation was as great as that of the tax-collector he had heard of who had simply left his counter. He, too, could follow him. But the eyes of the seer had scarcely met his. It had been a shock to be so disregarded; he himself had spent that night in the rock-tomb. The tomb had been a replica of the cave, further on the hill-side, where he had first tasted the ecstasy of communion, the red wine, shared with his common soldiers. He had been one of them, they had accepted him— would this man? Jesus had not noticed him, he supposed, being a Roman—anyhow, how could the young man know that he, Fabius, had turned the tempest of vituperation, on Golgotha? Yet if he were a seer, he must know. Had his powers gone from him? Had he paid the debt of the prophet, was he now in some sort of coma? Had he forgotten that past?

Fabius wanted one word. For that, he would have laid

down his shield, his sword, at the feet of a King.

He realised with a shock of psychic perception that Veronica was in the same predicament. They had both been left out.

Suddenly, as if mindful of inattention, of discourtesy, he said to Veronica, answering her spoken question, "Yes. They got off."

Fabius was seated opposite Veronica, telling the story.

"The carter was unsuspicious. The sailors had been warned. It was his feet that struck me. Suddenly the ignominy of it came over me, when I saw that he couldn't stand on his feet. Everything else was easy. The wind was as if prearranged. Everything was like that."

"Yes," Veronica answered, "it was. It was pre-arranged that I woke just then and came to you in the courtyard. It was arranged that you should be there." Now a sense of responsibility seemed to slip from her. Consciously she was now, just horribly tired. She even thought of the most ordinary matters, where was Bes? Sometimes the hall-servants nursed him in their quarters, still under the impression that Bes was some sort of glorified small cat. He would snatch at a small bird they proffered him, and tear it like a tiger. Animals—all this tearing of bird by beast, yet *not one falls*. It was all a tangle. Maybe, there was a clue in it, somewhere. For one moment, standing in the outer courtyard, all had seemed clear. Every layer of consciousness converged to one point. Now, she was like many points of light, flickering. Her mind felt like a wavering torch, that drops sparks. Her thinking returned to normal and she found it a relief to be so frankly hungry. If she could eat now. She said, "You must be hungry."

She told the servant by her door, that she wanted something brought here. She wanted fruit, wine. Wine—white or
red? She wanted both. She even specified those rarely used
crystal goblets. She wanted packed snow in a bowl. Her throat
suddenly felt intolerably dry and parched. She wanted the
fruit at once: ripe apricots or an Egyptian melon, brought by
that last boat. She felt as a starved animal must feel, she was
shaking with fatigue and nervous exhaustion. She visualised
the Prophet feeling like that, terribly tired, terribly hungry,
thirsty. Perhaps, after all, he was not so far off, in sympathy.
But she must stop thinking of him. That ray of light would be
concentrated again, and she would forget that she was ever
tired. There is an exhuastion that surpasses exhaustion, when
one feels numb or frozen. She had never been so tired.

Fabius thought, "It's an enchantment, I suppose it can't last
forever." The goblet, as he lifted it, caught prismatic light and
he saw the anemones that he had stooped to, shining black
almost against white narcissus. The narcissus he had bound,
in that cave, was like snow. He had laid it against the
Prophet's forehead, against clotted blood … just as those
eyelids wavered. Fabius didn't meet those eyes. Everything
was symbolical. Even the linen that was thrown across the
body, seemed to take lines, like carved stone. Yet the crippled
figure, standing in stark sunlight, had seemed intolerably human. He and Veronica were responsible for that. If they had
let the man hang there, his pain would now be over. But it is
over—Fabius shouted within himself, it is over. Human pain
is nothing to the inhuman, that terrible insanity of union
with the impossible. The man would be ordinary now, with

an ordinary companion. Bread would taste different. Bread would be just bread to him, while to them—Fabius broke a crisp loaf. To us? Has he bequeathed to us his terrible discovery of the unity of all things? Its symbol? Fabius supposed, when his fatigue passed, he would see things again in their orderly dimension.

Yet what was that? He began thinking with two minds, he saw everything two-fold, like seeing itself and its-self, reflected in clear water; he did not know which was the real image. Then he did knew. The two came together as he held his goblet a second time, to Veronica, who had dismissed the servant and was herself proffering him the flagon. The wine did flow out like red blood. He supposed between Mithra and this Jesus, he had been drawn into some sacred cycle. Sacred, it would go on forever.

He saw now that Veronica was Veronica, an ordinary woman, as ordinary as that girl who strode ahead of the ox-cart. At a bend in the road, they had fastened the cart with two waiting horses, the oxen's pace was too slow. Fabius had been impatient, there was always chance of discovery. He left the soldiers in charge of the oxen, indicated to the woman (Mnevis, Veronica had called her) that there was room for her in the wagon. She refused it.

The wide wheel-rim had crushed sweet-smelling herbs. They had brushed occasional low-sweeping branches of oleander. He surmised the water-courses had not yet run dry. It was still spring. Later, this would be a desert. Small birds whirred up like insects. The locusts already shrilled with an intimation of early summer. Fabius saw summer. Then every-thing dropped off; he was simply trudging by an ox-cart chaf-ing his two horses; they were too fine-bred for this work. The horses fretted in the unsuitable harness. Fabius himself had stalked forward to quiet the outer grey one. It was then, he caught the girl looking at him. Her eyes had a far-away dazed look, but that might be the sudden flood of sunlight. He sur-mised, sensed, from the throb in her bare throat, that she could sing.

"I think your—friend—that singing-girl could sing."

How long ago, was it that they had quarrelled about Mnevis? It was another world, that quarrel. It had a heavy "padded" atmosphere about it, it did not ring true. Now Veronica met his acknowledgment with a swift smile. Some-thing to her, came true then. It was Fabius.

Now all the painful flames and dying sparks in her were caught up in a new burning. She believed—what did she be-lieve? She believed that she had been right. Now she did not question her act. Surely the Prophet was human, he would have time now (as would she) for all the things that had es-caped him. To burn with so high, so pure, so concentrated a flame, is to burn out. He had burnt out, as had she. There was an end to psychic endurance, somewhere, a beginning. Spring is too beautiful, wild white narcissus is too beautiful. Jesus had been too beautiful. He knew nothing of Greek moderation, Roman pragmatism. He burnt up and out to that impossible divinity, and he with his love would have shared with all men—the impossible. O yes—he was impossible.

"Why yes – *God*," she said. White wine had poured life into her, like drinking air. It was tasting high mountain-air, listening to the flight of birds at dawn, that dawn. It was so few days ago that it had happened (three?) but already Jesus had created a new heaven, a new earth; merely, she said to herself, by being beautiful. She wanted to say this aloud. Instead she said, "I think something of that woman's song is – is contagious. I've caught it."

Fabius knew that something of the man's faith was contagious. What did it matter whether God, that Father of this new poet, or the Capitoline Jupiter or Zeus of the Hellenes, lived or didn't? The thing was to enjoy the perfection of this God's creation, the perfection of scent, of taste, of weariness, of rest, of endeavour. They had done something. He and Veronica – yes, and Pilate – had done something.

They had created a new world, because in the eyes of the populace, they had murdered a poet; through them, a poet still lived. Poetry, he thought, with inner lilt of conviction, is living. Jesus had taught that. Fabius had formerly thought the man's gesture affected, that manner of casually trusting epigrams and fine phrases to his followers, artificial. But no – Jesus had no time to write, he was so full of living.

And what had he taught? What had he done really? He had broken down barriers, so that all beauty flowed now in one channel. O, if only that Prophet, Fabius thought, could really found a new religion! Fantastically, his mind plunged forward into some future of perfection, where those words rang true. Why, he thought, what an inheritance; to have all the past to draw on, all those fantastic shapes and images of which Veronica spoke, bee and chick, from those temple-walls in Egypt, blending with an actual re-created present.

This Jesus had given new shape to the vine, the vine in

blossom, in fruit; he was a second Homer. Maligned by his people, he had spoken of love and the outcast woman in words, more exquisite than Ovid or Propertius. He had recognised the secret life, growing in the flower-petal, the bird-wing, the fish, moving lazy fin under clear water. Every simple object had its mutual shape in some other-world, some eternal world, of an eternal and a perfect Father. In the gross and imperfect, he had so perfectly sensed perfection, that many a cripple had straightened as he passed, many a derelict had grown whole, in his mere shadow. "If," said Fabius, "we could combine this Jesus with these others—" Veronica said, "—so I was thinking."

She had been thinking in her old fervid manner, then realised something was breaking in her head. It was an actual sensation. She thought, a lily must feel like that at the exact second that the sun pierces its closed leaf. This is a miracle, yes, this is a miracle. She remembered Memnonius and his earlier regret that she was a flower infolded. It seemed, she could hear it—as she had heard, that weary day in her room— a voice speaking. It said, "Veronica."

"I am Veronica," said Veronica, realising at last, that she was that person.

THE END